TRADI

Val took a deep b_____
before she lost her nerve. "Jason," she whispered,
her eyes focused on the nature movie their class
was watching. "Remember yesterday during lunch,
when I started to tell you something, and David
interrupted us?"

"Uh-huh." Jason was leaning so close she could
feel the warmth of his arm through his sleeve.

Val squirmed. His nearness was making her
stomach feel fluttery. "Well, my best friend Petey
is kind of . . . she'd like to . . ." Val stopped and
bit her lip. *There are no right words to ask the
boy I would like to date if he'll go to the dance
with my best friend!*

"Yeah?" Jason said encouragingly with a smile.

"Petey wanted me to ask you if you'd go to the
Valentine's Day dance with her." Val said in a
whispered rush. "I mean, if you're interested, then
she'll ask you."

Jason stared at the screen, where the whooping
cranes were winding up their courtship dance
with a furious flutter of wings.

"Sorry." Jason looked at her intently. "It's not
Petey I want to go to the dance with," he said
quietly.

Val felt sorry for her friend and for herself. It
definitely sounded as if Jason was interested in
somebody else. Her stomach constricted with a
sharp stab of jealousy. *Who was she?*

Bantam titles in the Sweet Dreams series. Ask your bookseller for any of the following titles you have missed:

Trading Hearts

Susan Blake

BANTAM BOOKS
TORONTO · NEW YORK · LONDON · SYDNEY · AUCKLAND

RL 6, IL age 11 and up

TRADING HEARTS
A Bantam Book/November 1990
Reprinted 1991
Reprinted 1995

Cover photo by Pat Hill

ISBN 0-553-27719-7

Published simultaneously in the United States and Canada

Printed and bound in Great Britain by
Cox & Wyman Ltd, Reading, Berkshire.

Trading Hearts

Chapter One

"How many more of these hearts do you think we'll have to cut out?" Val Cassidy asked, staring at the stack of red paper on the floor in front of her. She dropped her scissors and shook her fingers wearily. It felt like she'd already done at least a thousand.

Petey Boyd grinned at her from across the room, where she was sitting cross-legged on her bed, surrounded by a heap of red paper scraps. "Only three hundred to go," Petey told her. "I've been keeping track." Indigo Jones, Petey's dark blue parrakeet, was perched on her shoulder, nibbling delicately at her blond ponytail.

"Three hundred *more*?" Val asked unbelievingly, brushing her dark bangs out of her eyes and stretching her aching arms. "What's the dance committee trying to do—completely wallpaper the gym with these things?"

Petey laughed. "Good question."

With a squawk and a flap of his wings, Indigo Jones flew off Petey's shoulder and landed on Val's head. Val waved him off. "Really, Petey, don't you think it's a bit much to let your birds fly around loose when you've got company?" she said crossly. "I just washed my hair this morning."

Petey looked around the room. "Company?" she asked, pretending to be offended. "Who's company? I thought you were my best friend." She got up to open the birdcage, and the parakeet obligingly flew in to join his mate, Princess Leia. "That's okay, Indigo," Petey crooned tenderly. "Val didn't mean to be nasty. She's in a foul mood this afternoon because she'd rather be outside making a snowman."

Val smiled sheepishly. "Sorry," she muttered. "I guess I am kind of bummed today."

She got up and went to look out Petey's window. Fat white flakes were drifting lazily from a pewter-gray sky, blurring the school bus tracks in the snow that blanketed the lane. Bummed wasn't exactly the word for the way she felt, she thought. She was undecided about something—something important—and it was making her restless.

"Look," Val said, thrusting her hands into

the pockets of her jeans, "it's still snowing and Mom won't expect me home for another half hour. How about if we stopped cutting out hearts and went outside? The Valentine's Day dance isn't for a couple of weeks yet. We've got plenty of time to finish making decorations. Let's go throw snowballs or something."

Petey turned around to open another of the four cages that sat on a long shelf under the other window. Petey was crazy about birds—about animals of all kinds, really. Her walls were covered with wildlife posters, and a dozen stuffed animals sat on her bed. She wanted to be a veterinarian someday. It was a passion that Val had never quite understood, but she had to admit that she admired Petey's dedication. That was Petey for you, she thought, watching her friend put fresh birdseed into a plastic cup. Absolutely single-minded, and practical down to her fingernails. That was why Petey was always chosen to do things like manage the costumes for the drama club production and cut out hearts for the dance decorations.

Petey was being as practical as ever today. "But if we quit now, it will be even harder to get started again," she pointed out, closing the cage door. "After the hearts are done, you know, we've got to cut out all those stupid

3

cupids." She giggled and settled back on the bed with her scissors.

"What I want to know, Alberta Boyd," Val said blackly, sitting back down on the rug, "is who volunteered us to do all this?"

"And what *I* want to know, Valerie Cassidy," Petey retorted, "is what's bugging you these days? You've been acting weird for at least a week—no, make that a month. You must have something on your mind that you haven't told me about."

Val hesitated. She and Petey had been friends for a very long time, practically forever. Living outside of town the way they did, quite a distance from everybody else in their class and only a five-minute walk from each another, they spent almost all their free time together. They were as close as sisters, and they told each other everything.

Well, almost *everything,* Val thought, a trifle guiltily. The truth was that she did have something really special that she hadn't shared with Petey.

His name was Jason. Jason Talbot.

And what Val was so undecided about was whether she should invite him to the Valentine's Day Turn-About Dance.

Val picked up the scissors again and slowly began to cut out another heart. Why hadn't she told Petey about Jason? She'd never felt

4

like this about a boy before. Oh, there'd been silly little crushes, like the one she'd had on Marvin Whitkind freshman year, or the year before that on Rusty Craig. She and Petey had talked for hours and hours about them. And the first time Marvin Whitkind had kissed her good-night, she'd dashed into the house and called Petey immediately, even though it was after ten o'clock. The two of them had giggled over the details until her father had made her hang up.

But this time it was different. *Jason* was different. He'd only transferred to Anderson Mill High that fall, and already he was involved with all kinds of school activities. He'd joined the computer club and he'd just been named associate director of the drama club's production of *The Trip to Bountiful*. He'd organized the sophomore class car wash almost single-handedly, and everybody was saying that Jason Talbot would make a great class president next year. And on top of everything else, he was good-looking, with sandy-red hair, green eyes, and a warm, friendly smile that showed dimples in his cheeks.

But what made Val's feelings so hard to talk about, even to Petey, was the total impossibility of anything ever really coming of them. Val had thought about it from all sides. It just wasn't possible that somebody as ter-

5

rific as Jason Talbot would be interested in *her*. After all, with her short, dark brown hair, brown eyes, nondescript nose, and no particular talents, she was a *very* ordinary person. Not exactly the kind of girl that Jason Talbot would say yes to if she asked him to the Valentine's Day dance. He'd always been friendly enough when he saw her in class, but she knew it would never be anything more than that.

Val sighed and reached for another piece of construction paper. No, she wouldn't say anything to Petey about Jason. Not just yet, anyway. Talking about him would only get her hopes up—where really none existed.

Petey sniffed. "Well, if you're not going to tell me what's on your mind," she said, "I guess I'll just have to tell you what's on mine." In one of the cages under the window, a gray cockatiel began to squawk loudly, and Petey yelled, "Shut up, Taco!" Taco gave a last *"Yawk!"* and the racket subsided.

Val looked up at her friend with relief. "Okay, what's up?"

Petey looked a bit uncomfortable. "Promise you won't laugh?"

"Of course," Val said. She crossed her heart with two fingers and then held them up, the way they'd done ever since grade school. "Why should I laugh?"

6

"Because," Petey said. She shook her head, smiling. Her blue eyes were twinkling. "I'm in love."

"In love!" Val exclaimed. She scrambled to her feet and ran over to the bed to flop down beside Petey. "Oh, Petey, that's *wonderful*! Who is he?" He had to be somebody pretty special. Petey had lots of friends who were boys, but she'd never had a boyfriend.

"I'll give you a hint," Petey said. She clasped her arms around her knees with a dreamy smile. "He's the most terrific boy in the entire sophomore class. He's good-looking, popular, everybody likes him—"

Val got up on her knees and shook Petey by the shoulders. "Who *is* he?" she demanded.

Petey grinned. "Need another hint? He's the associate director of *The Trip to Bountiful*."

Val sat back on her heels. She could hardly believe what she had heard. "*Jason?*" she asked incredulously. "Jason Talbot?"

"Isn't he wonderful?" Petey squealed, hugging herself.

Val frowned. Her best friend was in love with Jason? Did he care for Petey, too? Val had never seen the two of them together, but they were both in drama club. Petey had plenty of chances to talk to him, to work with him. Val felt a sudden flash of envy. But Petey was waiting for an answer to her question.

7

"Yes, he is wonderful," Val said slowly. "But . . ." She swallowed, trying to keep the misery from showing in her eyes. Now she could *never* tell Petey how she felt about Jason. She couldn't tell anybody—especially Jason!

"I know." Petey heaved a mournful sigh. She rolled onto her back and folded her arms under her head. "There's a great, big, horrible *but* right in the middle, isn't there? I mean, he's such a great guy, and so popular— but he doesn't know I like him."

"He doesn't?" Val asked, hoping Petey couldn't hear the relief in her voice.

Petey shook her head and sat up again, looking eager. "That's where *you* come in, Val."

"Me?" Val stared at her friend blankly. "What do you mean, that's where *I* come in?"

Petey reached for her hand. "Well, you know the Valentine's Day dance is coming up, right?"

"Of course I know about that, silly," Val said. She gestured toward the construction paper on the floor. "Why else would I be cutting out all these stupid red-paper hearts?"

Petey grinned widely. "What I want you to do, Val, is to find out whether Jason would go to the dance with me if I asked him."

Val pulled her hand away quickly. "Now,

just a minute," she said firmly, "I'm not going to—"

"You don't have to actually ask him to the dance," Petey interrupted. "I'll do that. I mean, I will if you say that he says it's okay." She frowned a little. "Did I say that right?"

"I get the general idea," Val said. "Listen, Petey, I don't think—"

"I know," Petey said ruefully. "I'm really putting you on the spot, Val, but there's nobody I trust more than you. If it were anyone else but Jason, I'd just go ahead and ask him, no sweat. But I'm . . . well, Jason makes me feel *shy*. I mean, it's not him—he's really nice. It's *me*. I get all tongue-tied around him, and I stammer and stutter like an idiot." She paused and turned a pleading glance to Val. "I can ask him myself," she said, "as long as I know in advance that he'll say yes. I guess I just don't have any confidence when it comes to love. Do you know what I mean?"

Slowly, Val nodded. "I know what you mean," she said. "If I were you I'd—I'd probably feel the same way." If she'd been more confident, she would have asked Jason herself by now. She'd put off asking him for exactly the same reason. Because she was afraid he'd say no.

"So you'll do it?" Petey asked anxiously.

Val thought of all the good times she and

Petey had enjoyed together, the games, the laughter, the advice, the sharing of secrets. If she said no, it might make a difference between them. How could she explain her refusal to Petey without telling her how she felt about Jason?

She took a deep breath. "I guess so."

"Oh, thank you, thank you," Petey said, throwing her arms around Val. "I knew I could count on you! Val Cassidy, you're the very best friend in the whole world!"

Chapter Two

"Val! Wilson! Breakfast is ready," Val's mother called from the foot of the stairs.

"Okay, Mom," Val called back. "I'll be down in a minute."

Val stared at herself in the bathroom mirror as she ran a brush through her dark brown hair and finished putting on her eye makeup. There were dark circles under her eyes—a dead giveaway that she hadn't slept very well. She'd tossed and turned half the night, thinking about Petey and Jason and trying to imagine how she was going to approach him. She grinned weakly at her image in the mirror. What in the world would she say to the boy she'd love to date to find out if he liked her best friend? It was a terrible dilemma—the worst one of her whole life.

The bathroom doorknob rattled. "Hey, hurry

up, Val," her six-year-old brother, Wilson, pleaded. "Mom's yelling that I've got to comb my hair or I won't get any hot chocolate for breakfast."

Val opened the door and Wilson smiled at her. He was missing one tooth, right in the middle. "Anyway," he said, pushing through the door, "you're already pretty enough."

Val laughed. "You just made my day, Willie," she said affectionately, ruffling his curly blond hair as she left the bathroom.

In the kitchen, Mrs. Cassidy was pouring cereal into three earthenware bowls. "Hey," she said, eyeing the new blue floral-print blouse Val was wearing with her jeans. "You really look nice this morning. Something special going on at school?"

Val colored. "Sort of," she said evasively. She'd worn blue because she'd once overheard Jason say that it was his favorite color. She sat down at the round oak table. "Has Dad already gone to work?" Her father was a lawyer in Anderson Mill.

Mrs. Cassidy nodded and pulled aside the blue-and-white checked curtain at the window. Outside, the snow was still falling. "He left about a half hour ago. I think he was afraid that the snowplow might not have made it all the way to our corner."

Val sliced a banana into her bowl. "I don't suppose they've called off school?"

"Not a chance." Mrs. Cassidy poured her a cup of hot chocolate. "But you've still got fifteen minutes before the bus is due. And it'll probably be a little late this morning." She sat down at the table and looked directly at her daughter. "Val, is there something wrong at school?" she asked, sounding concerned. "You've been a little distracted lately. And this morning you look positively gloomy. Is there something on your mind that you'd like to talk about?"

Val looked up. "Well, actually, there is," she said, touched by the warmth in her mother's voice. And suddenly it all came spilling out. Her feelings about Jason, her conversation with Petey, and what Petey had asked her to do. Halfway through her story, Wilson came into the kitchen, but for once he didn't interrupt. He just sat in his chair and began to eat.

"So I told Petey I'd talk to him," Val said heavily. "But now I'm not exactly sure I did the right thing. Maybe I should refuse to talk to Jason for her. Or maybe I should just tell Petey the truth—even though it's a little late."

Her mother put her hand over Val's. "I think you're doing the right thing," she said with a little smile. "You know, sometimes you can't see very far ahead. You have to feel your way, one step at a time, and see what develops.

13

You and Petey have been friends for a very long time. I think you're right to value that friendship over the way you feel about Jason, and I'm proud of you for it. It might have been different if you'd spoken first, but . . ."

Val let out a glum sigh and went to the sink to rinse her cereal bowl. "I know. I guess I should have told her how I felt. But it's too late now."

Wilson drained his hot chocolate. "I'll *never* have a girlfriend," he announced firmly. "They're too much trouble."

Mrs. Cassidy leaned forward to pat him on the head. "Don't you think you're a little young to make a decision like that, Wilson?"

Wilson considered. "Well, maybe." He threw Val a sideways glance. "Maybe Petey could be my girlfriend, Val," he suggested helpfully. "*I* could take her to the dance."

Val had to laugh in spite of herself. "Now *that*," she said as she took her red coat off the hook by the door and shrugged into it, "might solve all my problems." She sat down and began to tug on her boots. "Come on, Willie. Last one out to the bus stop is the abominable snowman!"

Ten minutes later, the high school bus pulled up. As usual, there were only two kids on it so far, Petey and David MacIntosh. David was sitting behind the driver, absorbed

14

in his biology book. He looked up with a shy grin as Val took the seat beside Petey, then went back to his reading.

"Hi, Val," Petey said, looking bright and cheerful in her green jacket and jaunty beret. "Listen, I've been thinking about our talk yesterday afternoon." She leaned over and lowered her voice as the bus pulled to a stop and three senior girls got on. "*You* know."

Val felt a faint spark of hope. "You mean you've changed your mind?" she asked, unwinding her white wool muffler.

"No, of course not, silly," Petey said, frowning. She signaled secretly to the back of David's head. "You know that David is Jason's best friend," she whispered.

Val nodded. The two boys weren't very much alike: Jason was outgoing and handsome, while David was shy and studious, with owlish-looking glasses and a mouthful of braces. But they seemed to have become close friends in the few months Jason had been at Anderson Mill.

"So," Petey continued, with a cajoling smile, "wouldn't it be fun to double-date to the dance?"

"Double-date?" Val asked, frowning a little. She thought fleetingly of Jason. "Hey, wait a minute! *You're* the one who's looking for a date, remember? I'm not going to the dance."

"But that's just the point," Petey said triumphantly. "You could if you wanted to. You could ask David and we could all go together. Afterward we could go out for pizza and—"

"David? David MacIntosh?" Val exclaimed, bristling. Petey put a finger to her lips, glancing in David's direction, and Val lowered her voice. "Now, just a minute, Alberta Boyd," she said. "I agreed to try to find out if Jason would go to the dance with you. I didn't say anything about going to the dance myself. You can just cross that double-date idea right off your list." She folded her arms across her chest and slouched down in her seat, glaring straight ahead. For some reason, she felt like crying.

"What's wrong with David MacIntosh?" Petey asked. "I mean, once you get past the glasses and braces, he's really a nice-looking guy. And he's pretty smart, too. He's in my biology class and—"

"It doesn't have anything to do with glasses or braces or how nice David MacIntosh is or isn't," Val said crossly. "It has to do with me not wanting to go to the dance, that's all." She could feel the tears burning her eyes.

"Oh, come on," Petey coaxed. "I mean, it's not like getting engaged or anything, Val. It's just a dance. We could have a lot of fun together—the way we always do."

16

Val wanted more than anything to tell her friend why she couldn't go to the dance—with David or anybody else. She couldn't bear the thought of watching Jason hold Petey in his arms as they danced across the floor. Grimly, she pressed her lips shut and shook her head.

"Well, okay," Petey said contritely. "If that's the way you feel, I'll stop bugging you about it." She turned to look out the window at the snowy fields. "But I just don't understand you at all," she added, half under her breath.

The night before, Val had decided that it would be best to get her task over with in a hurry. That way, she wouldn't have to worry about it anymore. She still wasn't sure exactly what she should say to Jason. She'd probably have to walk right up to him, open her mouth, and hope for the best. It was all she could manage under the circumstances.

Val hurried to homeroom in order to catch Jason before the bell rang. But he was up front, talking to Mrs. Samuelson about something, and he didn't come back to his desk right away. When the period was over, he smiled and waved to her, but she dawdled a little, gathering up her books. By the time she was finally ready to leave, Jason was on his way out the door with a couple of other kids.

17

During second-period English, when Mrs. Hawkins started to write the assignment on the blackboard, Petey leaned over to ask Val if she'd talked to Jason yet.

Val shook her head. "I tried this morning," she said, "but he was busy." She felt a twinge of guilt, thinking about the way she'd dawdled after homeroom. Had she really tried hard enough to catch Jason? "I guess I'll catch him at lunch."

"Okay," Petey agreed. "I've got to talk to Mr. Howard about my dumb old math, anyway. I really bombed on that test this morning." She made a face. "At least I won't be around when you talk to Jason."

Val grinned. "You make it sound like I'm going to commit a murder or something."

"Well, that's what you *look* like," Petey retorted. "Really bummed out. Come on, Val, cheer up. Jason won't bite."

"Oh, yeah?" Val asked sarcastically. "Then how come you don't ask him yourself?"

"Because he might say no," Petey said. She opened her English book just as Mrs. Hawkins stopped writing and turned around from the blackboard.

At lunch, Val went through the salad line and then stood uncertainly, looking around the noisy, crowded cafeteria. All the tables

18

were taken, but Jason was nowhere to be seen. Val felt a distinct sense of relief flood through her. Maybe she could put off her chore a little while longer.

"Hi," said a voice at her elbow. "It's a real mob scene, huh? Are you looking for a place to sit?"

Val turned with a start. Jason Talbot was smiling down at her, his green eyes crinkling at the corners. Val's heart began to thump crazily.

"No, not exactly . . . I mean, yes," she stammered.

"Well, then, how about over there?" Jason asked, gesturing with the milk carton he held in his hand. "I've already put my tray on that table by the window. There's plenty of room."

"Okay, thanks," Val managed to say after a moment. She followed him over to the table and put her tray down.

Jason sat across from her. "Does it usually snow this hard around here?" he asked, looking out the window. The snow had stopped earlier that morning, but it had started again, and now there was a soft drift almost five feet high in front of the baseball backstop. Jason grinned, and she noticed how white and even his teeth were. "Down in Florida, where I come from, the sun is probably shining, and after school everybody'll go water-skiing. Have you ever been water-skiing?"

Val shook her head. "Only once," she confessed, relaxing a little. "I forgot to let go of the towrope."

"That's kind of hard on the nose," Jason said, chuckling. "Was that what made your nose turn up on the end?" Then, as if he was afraid he'd hurt her feelings, he added quickly, "I mean, it's really cute that way."

Val felt the red rise in her cheeks. "The snow must be quite a change from sand," she said, hoping to change the subject. She looked down at her plate and speared a piece of tomato with her fork, feeling his eyes on her.

"Well, all in all, I guess I like it," Jason replied. "At least my mom doesn't yell at me for tracking it onto the carpet."

Val laughed. "Just wait until March, when it gets all slushy and turns into yucky mud. Your mom will probably yell a *lot*." She took another bite of salad. It was wonderful to talk to Jason, and so easy, too. Why had she been afraid? Suddenly she remembered her mission. She was supposed to find out whether Jason would go to the dance with Petey.

She sighed. Well, there was no sense in putting it off any longer. And once she had discharged her duty to Petey, she could stop feeling guilty. "Jason," she began, "there's something I—"

"Hey, Val, do you know anything about—" he said at exactly the same time.

They laughed. "You first," Val said.

"No, you," he replied.

"No," Val insisted. She didn't want to ask about the dance, not just yet, anyway. After she'd asked her question, all the fun would be over. She'd no longer have any excuse to seek him out. "What were you going to say?"

Jason took a sip of his milk. "I was just wondering about the Valentine's Day dance," he said.

Val stared at him. The dance? Why had he brought that up? Had he read her mind?

"I mean," he said, shifting a little under her intense gaze, "is it going to be formal? Do people usually get dressed up?"

Val swallowed. "No. Yes. Well, I mean, it's not formal, but people do get kind of dressed up. Dresses and sports jackets, that sort of thing." She had to admit, even though she didn't want to, that this was the perfect opportunity to bring up Petey. "Listen, Jason," she said, "about the dance—"

"Hi, Jay. Hello, Val." A tray was set down on the table beside her, and she looked up, startled. It was David MacIntosh.

"Mind if I join you?" he asked, pulling up a chair. "I'm not interrupting anything vital, am I?"

Jason smiled at him, then leaned forward quickly. "What were you saying, Val?"

Val shook her head. She couldn't talk to Jason about the dance with David there. "Oh, nothing that can't wait a day or so. I'll talk to you later." She glanced down at her watch as if she'd suddenly remembered something important. "Oops, sorry," she said, getting up quickly. "I didn't realize how late it was. I've got to go."

For a second, she thought that Jason looked disappointed. Then he grinned. "Okay, see you later."

As she put her tray onto the conveyer belt, Val couldn't resist a last look over her shoulder. Jason and David were talking, their heads close together. Suddenly Jason looked up and waved at her, grinning widely. As Val left the cafeteria she chided herself for her wildly thudding heart and silly grin. Jason and Val together was just an impossible dream.

Chapter Three

"Hey, Val!" Petey called, waving her arms frantically. "Over here!"

Val pushed her way through the noisy, jostling crowd gathered on the front steps of the high school to wait for the school bus. It was early the next morning, and the two biology classes were getting together for a field trip to the local natural history museum.

"Hi," Val said breathlessly. "Wow, I was afraid I wasn't going to make it. I was late to homeroom and Mrs. Samuelson decided that I needed a lecture about punctuality."

"I was worried when you didn't get on the bus this morning," Petey said, pulling on her green mittens. She had a notebook tucked under her arm. "I'm so excited about this trip that I woke up early. Did you oversleep?"

"No, not really." Val shook her head, avoiding Petey's curious glance. "Dad was going in to the office a little later, so I decided to ride with him."

That was true, Val knew, but the real reason was that she'd known Petey was going to ask her if she'd talked with Jason yesterday and she wasn't sure what to say. She was definitely going to have to say something to Petey soon, though.

The bus pulled up, and the girls pushed their way into line with the other students.

"Did you try to call me last night?" Petey asked. "I had play practice after school, and then I had to go over to Aunt Catherine's with Mom. We didn't get back until ten o'clock." She sighed. "What a disaster. I didn't get my math homework done again, and Mr. Howard's going to *slaughter* me."

Val climbed on the bus and headed toward a vacant seat halfway back. "No, I didn't get a chance to call," she told Petey.

"Well, did you talk to him?" Petey demanded, sliding into the seat. "What did he say? Come on, Val, don't keep me in suspense!"

Val took a deep breath. "Actually, Petey, I—"

"Hi, Val! Hi, Petey."

It was Jason, with David MacIntosh at his heels. The two flopped into the empty seat behind Val and Petey, and Val's heart began turning idiotic flip-flops.

She glanced at Petey. Her friend's cheeks were bright red, and she looked almost panic-stricken. "Uh . . . good morning, Jason," Petey stammered, hunching down in her seat. She looked sideways at Val.

"What did he *say*?" she demanded in a fierce whisper. "Should I ask him?"

"I'm sorry, Petey," Val whispered back. "I didn't get a chance to find out. David came up and interrupted us just as I was about to ask him."

To Val's surprise, Petey looked relieved. "Oh," she said. "Well, that's okay. For a minute I was kind of worried."

Val stared at her friend. "What do you mean, it's okay? I thought you'd be really disappointed. Have you decided you're not interested in him after all?" she asked hopefully.

"No, of course not," Petey said, looking at her strangely. "I *am* disappointed—sort of." She grinned. "But it would be really embarrassing to sit in front of Jason like this all the way to the museum if he knew I was going to ask him to the dance, right?"

The biology teacher, Mrs. Robbins, assembled the students in the main lobby of the museum, then held up her hand for silence. "As you recall, everyone, we're here this morning to study birds. Right now," she continued, "we're going to see a film on bird courtship displays, and then we'll examine the museum's stuffed bird collection." She nodded toward a pair of double doors. "Okay, everybody. Let's find our seats in the auditorium."

"Where do you want to sit?" Val asked Petey as they entered the auditorium.

"How about over there?" she said, pointing.

Val's heart sank. Jason and David were sitting together, and there was an empty seat on each side of them. "Are you sure that's where you want to sit?" she asked doubtfully.

"Why not?" Petey said airily, tossing her ponytail. "Sitting next to Jason will give me a little practice—you know, for the dance." She giggled. "After all, I *am* going to have to talk to him *then,* right?"

"I guess so," Val replied reluctantly. "I suppose you want me to sit next to David."

Petey squeezed her arm and smiled happily as she turned to walk down the aisle. "Have I ever told you," she asked, "what a really terrific friend you are?"

David looked up in surprise as Val appeared beside him. "Hi," she said, gesturing toward the empty seat. "Uh, do you mind—?"

David shook his head and threw a quick look in the other direction, where Petey had sat down next to Jason.

Just as Val sat down, David jumped up.

"Sorry, I forgot something. I'll be right back." With that, he scrambled over Val's knees and hurried up the aisle to the back of the auditorium.

Val shrugged out of her coat, folded it on her lap, and stared at the screen as the lights dimmed. *Why did I let Petey talk me into this?* she thought. This scheme would never work.

Suddenly there was a flurry of movement to her right as somebody moved down the row to the seat next to her. Val relaxed a little and settled back to enjoy the movie. At that moment someone stepped on her foot and she pulled it back with a half-smothered yelp of surprise.

"Sorry," a voice muttered. "I couldn't see where I was going. I didn't mean to step on you."

"No problem." Val concentrated on the screen and tried not to think of Petey and Jason together.

"I hope you don't mind about me switching seats," the boy next to her whispered again, leaning closer to Val. His breath brushed her neck and she shivered involuntarily when she suddenly recognized the voice. *Jason!* "I got the idea that David wanted to sit beside Petey, so—"

"He wanted to do *what*?" Val whispered

27

back, not sure that she'd heard correctly. Val leaned forward and peered to her right. Two places down, David was in Jason's old seat next to Petey. Petey was staring at the parrots on the screen with an expression of intense and utter frustration.

"He wanted to sit beside Petey," Jason repeated. "You know, to try to get to know her better."

"Oh," Val said, "I see." *David* was interested in *Petey*? She considered that idea for a minute. The two of them were alone together on the bus for a quarter of an hour or so every morning, before Val got on. But David usually had his face buried in a book. He was pretty shy. Petey probably didn't even know that he wanted to get better acquainted with her.

Val tried to collect her thoughts, but it was hard, with Jason sitting so close to her. His hand was on the armrest between them, his fingers almost touching her sleeve. Suddenly it occurred to her that now would be the perfect time to tell Jason about Petey. The best part was that it was very dark in the auditorium, so he couldn't see her clearly. That way, if her face betrayed her real feelings for him, it wouldn't matter. All she had to do was keep her voice steady.

On the screen, the scene had shifted to a

shallow, reed-bordered bay. A pair of whooping cranes were whirling and prancing on their stalky legs. The male had his wings lifted high, like an umbrella, and he was making a loud yawking noise. The kids in the auditorium were laughing at his comic antics. Down at the end of the row, Petey was hunched over her notebook, trying to scribble something in the dark.

Val took a deep breath. She had to do it now, before she lost her nerve. "Jason," she whispered, her eyes on the screen, "remember yesterday, when I started to tell you something, and David came over?"

"Uh-huh." Jason's shoulder was now against hers, so Val could feel the warmth of his arm through his sleeve. His nearness was making her stomach feel fluttery.

"What I wanted to tell you," she said, steadying her voice, "has to do with the Valentine's Day dance. You know that the girls ask the boys?"

Jason half-turned toward her. "Yeah," he said close to her ear. "I know."

Val squirmed, wishing that he wouldn't lean so near to her. It was making things harder. "Well, Petey's kind of . . . that is, she'd like . . ." She stopped and bit her lip. She should have planned better what she was going to say. If she wasn't careful, she was going to mess everything up, or say something she shouldn't.

"Yeah?" Jason said encouragingly.

"Petey wanted me to ask you if you'd be interested in going to the dance with her," Val said in a whispered rush. "I mean, if you are, then she'll ask you."

Jason stared at the screen, where the whooping cranes were winding up their courtship dance with a furious flutter of wings. Finally he turned back to Val, just as the screen brightened to another scene. Val could clearly see his handsome face, the line of his cheek, the firm angle of his jaw.

"I guess I have to say no, Val," he said very quietly.

"Oh," Val said dully. "Petey's going to be disappointed."

Jason was still looking at her intently. "It's not Petey I want to go to the dance with," he said.

Val felt a flurry of conflicting emotions. She was relieved that she'd fulfilled her promise to Petey, but she also felt sorry for her friend. And it definitely sounded as if Jason was interested in somebody else. Her stomach constricted with a stab of jealousy. *Who was she?*

At that moment, incredibly, Jason reached for her hand. His fingers tightened on hers.

"The truth is," he said, "I was hoping *you'd* ask me."

Chapter Four

At first, Val wasn't sure she'd heard him correctly. Maybe she was imagining the whole thing. Jason Talbot wanted to go to the dance with *her*? It seemed impossible, but Jason's hand was still holding hers. Then he suddenly let it go. For an instant, Val felt a sharp regret—it had felt so good to have Jason's hand on hers. But what if Petey had seen the two of them holding hands? She quickly stuck her hand under the coat on her lap, still feeling the wonderful, tingling warmth of his fingers.

"You want to go with *me*?" she whispered unbelievingly. Something seemed to fizz and sparkle inside her, making her feel amazingly light and buoyant.

Jason nodded. "Uh-huh." There was a pause, and he grinned. "Is that such a surprise? Yesterday, when David interrupted us, I thought maybe you were getting ready to ask me." His grin widened. "I was all set to say yes, in case you didn't notice."

"I didn't," Val said, wishing that she'd paid more attention. "Actually, I *was* trying to ask you—but for Petey." When she thought of her friend, the fizzy feeling went away and she felt let down, like a limp balloon. "She . . . she really likes you."

"I like her, too," Jason said. "She's doing a terrific job with the costumes for the play, and she's a nice girl. But I'm not interested in her as a girlfriend." He nodded to his right. "That's David's department."

"David?"

"Yeah. He's got a real crush on Petey. That's why he wanted to trade seats with me. He's trying to engineer things so she'll ask him to the dance."

"Oh, no!" Val exclaimed out loud. Her hand flew to her mouth.

"Oh, yes," Jason said, chuckling. "He's been thinking about this for a long time, almost all year, to tell the truth. But he's sort of shy, you know, and it took him a long time to work up the nerve just to sit beside her." He grinned again. "I predict, though, that things will go pretty fast. He's the kind of guy who knows what he wants."

32

At that moment, Mrs. Robbins came up behind them and tapped them both on the shoulder. "Jason," she whispered sternly, "if you want to talk to Valerie, you'll have to wait until the film is over. You're disturbing the others around you." She frowned at Val. "Really, Valerie, I'm surprised at you."

"Excuse me, ma'am," Val said, with a meek nod. When Mrs. Robbins had left, she sneaked a look at Jason and giggled nervously. He glanced over his shoulder to make sure that Mrs. Robbins had gone back up the aisle, and whispered, "If you ask me, the two of *them* don't look very disturbed." He gestured toward Petey and David. "In fact, they look like they're both into this movie in a very major way."

Val looked over. Petey was leaning forward, hurriedly scribbling something in the notebook on her lap. David was whispering something to her and holding a pocket penlight so that she could see what she was writing.

"Do you think maybe they'll work something out?" Jason asked. "In time for the dance, I mean."

"I don't know," Val replied doubtfully. She sighed. "I don't think she'll go with David when she's got her heart set on going with you."

"You still haven't said," Jason pointed out

33

after a moment, "how *you* feel about going with *me*." He paused and cleared his throat. "I guess I'm going out on a limb to say that I'm available, if you decide you want to ask me."

Val drew in her breath. "I did," she said, so softly that she wasn't sure whether Jason could hear her. "I mean I do want to ask you."

"Hey, Val," he exclaimed, "that's great!" He reached for her hand, still hidden under her coat.

"No," she said miserably, feeling the tears rise in her throat. "It isn't." She pulled her hand away.

He turned to face her. "What do you mean, it isn't?" he asked, looking bewildered.

"Because I *can't* ask you to the dance," she burst out, so loudly that two girls in the row ahead of them turned around and stared. Val quickly glanced in Petey's direction, but her friend seemed not to have heard.

"Why not?" Jason demanded when the girls had turned back around. "I mean, if you really want to go with me, why can't we do it?"

"Because of Petey," Val said thickly. "I mean, Petey and I have been friends—*best* friends—since grade school. If I went to the dance with you, she'd probably never speak to me again, and I couldn't blame her. I just couldn't *do* that to her, Jason. I couldn't hurt Petey, no matter how much I wanted to go with you."

For a long moment, Jason was silent. "Yes," he said finally, "I think you probably couldn't. Maybe that's one of the things I like about you. You're always so honest, and you say what you think. You're really a straight shooter."

Val leaned back against the seat, trying to clear her mind of her jumbled thoughts. It was all such a mess! She wanted to go to the dance with Jason, and—wonder of wonders!—Jason wanted to go with her. In fact, it seemed like he'd been checking her out for some time now, which she found hard to believe. But Petey wanted to go with Jason too, and David wanted to go with Petey. She sighed. How would they *ever* get things sorted out?

"Listen," Jason whispered in her ear. "If we could fix things so that Petey decided she really wanted to go to the dance with David, would you go with me?"

Val sighed. *Would* she? "Yes," she said. "Of course I would. But how are we going to do that?"

"To be honest, I don't have a clue," Jason confessed. "But I'll come up with something. And in the meantime, maybe you could talk to Petey—you know, kind of sound her out on whether she likes David. Maybe you could even nudge her a little bit in his direction."

"I don't really think that's a good idea " Val said. "I mean, if she doesn't *want* to go with David, it's not fair to force her into anything. I don't want her to go with him unless it's her own idea."

"No, of course not," Jason agreed. "That wouldn't be fair. I'm not asking you to do anything you're uncomfortable with. But you will talk to her about him, won't you? I mean, I really hope we can go to the dance together, Val."

Val's heart did another flip. "I do too," she said.

Up on the screen, the music swelled to a climax, then the lights began to come on and everybody started talking noisily. At the other end of the row, Petey stood up, closed her notebook, and signaled to Val to meet her at the back of the auditorium.

Val was turning to walk up the aisle with her coat under her arm when she felt Jason's hand on her sleeve. "I'll get to work on this right away," he said. "Maybe I can figure something out."

"Good luck," Val said. And she meant it. As she walked up the aisle, she thought how much things had changed during the half

36

hour they'd been watching the movie. She'd discovered something she hadn't thought possible, something that could come true only in her dreams. Jason Talbot liked her! And she'd solved one problem—how to talk to Jason about Petey. But now she had another problem to solve—an even *bigger* one. How was she going to encourage Petey to like David enough to ask him to the dance?

Petey was waiting just outside the doors. "Wasn't that a great film?" she exclaimed, waving her notebook. "I really got a lot of good stuff, and David was telling me about some things that weren't even in the film, so I got that too."

"That's great," Val said. "I saw him helping you out with his flashlight," she added, watching Petey closely. "Do you like him?"

Petey shrugged without changing expression. "Sure," she said. "I don't know David very well, but he seems to be an okay guy—at least where animals are concerned."

"*Just* where animals are concerned?" Val prompted.

"Yeah," Petey said. "Why?" She paused and gave Val a curious look. "Are you reconsidering my idea about asking him to double-date with Jason and me?"

Val shook her head vigorously and Petey laughed. They walked toward the display area where the stuffed bird collection was kept, continuing their conversation. "I never did figure out why those guys traded seats, did *you*?" Petey asked. "I was all set to talk to Jason, and the next thing I knew, David was sitting next to me."

"Musical chairs, I guess." Val laughed weakly. "Or maybe David just wanted to be near you."

Petey ignored her comment, and Val felt a stab of disappointment. It was obvious that she wasn't at all attracted to David.

"Well, at least it gave you a chance to talk to Jason," Petey said. She turned to Val. "Were you able to find out anything? Does he like me? Will he go to the dance with me if I ask him?"

Val cleared her throat nervously. She couldn't tell Petey the truth, but she didn't want to lie.

"Yeah, I did talk to him a little," she said, choosing her words carefully. "At least until Mrs. Robbins gave us orders to be quiet." Val hunched her shoulders, not looking at Petey. "Well, I think he might possibly be interested in the dance, but it's hard to say for sure. Maybe we should wait and ask him again in a couple of days."

It wasn't exactly a lie, she told herself. He *was* interested, although not in Petey. And it *was* hard to say for sure how things were going to turn out.

Petey nodded. "He's playing hard to get, huh?" she asked. "That's funny. I didn't think Jason Talbot was that kind of guy." She made a face. "Actually, I sort of hoped we wouldn't have to play games. I hate the idea of trying to make people do something they don't want to do." She looked anxiously at Val. "It's not like that, is it?"

"No, that's not exactly it," Val answered.

"Well, then, what exactly is it?" Petey demanded. "Is he interested in somebody else?"

Val chewed the corner of her lip. "I think we just have to work our way through this a step at a time," she said, remembering the words her mother had used, "and see what develops."

Petey sighed. "Okay, whatever you say," she replied. She rolled her eyes upward. "I'll tell you one thing, though. This dating business sure is hard on the nerves. And if it's this hard for a girl to ask a guy for one little date, think how tough it must be for a guy to ask a girl to get married."

"Hmmm," Val muttered. Petey was right, in more ways than she knew. The dating business *was* hard on the nervous system. Especially when you were stuck between your very best friend and a guy you liked more than any other guy in your whole life!

Petey reached for Val's hand and squeezed it. "If anybody can convince Jason to go to the dance, Val, it'll be you. There's nobody else in the entire world that I trust as much as I trust you. Why, I'd trust you with my very life."

"Thanks, Petey," Val said with a twisted grin. She wished fervently that she could just go somewhere and hide for a month. She was beginning to wish she had never heard of the Valentine's Day dance!

Chapter Five

"Well, you don't look quite so gloomy today," Mrs. Cassidy teased as Val came to the breakfast table on Friday morning. "With that yellow sweater, you look as sunny as a field of daffodils."

Val laughed as she helped herself to some bacon from the plate in the middle of the table. "Well, part of my problem is solved, at least," she said.

"Which part?" her mother asked as she poured two glasses of orange juice. She handed one to Wilson, who was hunched over a plate of pancakes.

"The part about who Jason Talbot wants to go to the dance with," Val answered. She poured syrup on her pancakes. "But the rest is a bigger puzzle than ever."

"Who does Jason want to go to the dance

with?" Mrs. Cassidy asked, sitting down and buttering a piece of toast for herself.

Val sighed. "Believe it or not, he says he'd like to go with—me!" She smiled a little crookedly. Here she was, sighing over the very thing that she'd have given *anything* for just a few days before. Life was so crazy sometimes.

Her mother looked up, startled. "That's great," she said. "But that does complicate things, doesn't it?"

"You said it," Val said. "And to make it even more complicated, it turns out that David MacIntosh—Jason's best friend—would like to go to the dance with Petey."

"Does Petey know any of this?"

"Not yet," Val said. She glanced at her mother, trying to decipher her reaction. "Jason says we should try to figure out how to get Petey to *want* to go to the dance with David. That way, I could go with him."

Mrs. Cassidy frowned. "Are you sure it's a good idea to try to manipulate people, Val? I know you like Jason, but don't let that blind you to—"

Wilson looked up. "Manipulate?" he asked curiously, with his mouth full of pancakes. "What does it mean to manipulate?"

"You're manipulating people," Val explained, "when you try to get them to do something they don't want to do just because you want them to do it." She hesitated. Was that what she was doing to Petey?

"Oh, yeah, I know," Wilson said with an emphatic nod. "It's like when you and Mom manipulate me into bed at night when I don't want to go."

Val and her mother laughed. "Well, it's something like that," Val said. She turned to her mother, sobering. "No, I *don't* want to manipulate Petey, but what if she'd really like David but she doesn't know it? Maybe we'll be doing her a big favor to help her figure it out."

"Now that," Mrs. Cassidy said gently, "sounds like a first-class rationalization to me."

Wilson looked up again, his forehead furrowed. He had syrup on his nose. "What's a first-class ra-tion-a-lization?" he asked. "If Val gets one, can I have one too?"

"Eat your pancakes," Val and her mother replied in unison. And then they all laughed.

Mr. Hofsteader, who taught fourth-period history, was one of Val's favorite teachers. What was more, she liked American history and she always got an A in it. But this morning she couldn't concentrate on anything the teacher was saying. Petey was sitting on one side of her, and Jason was sitting on the other, looking very handsome in a green sweater that matched the color of his eyes. Val was feeling very much in the middle.

While Mr. Hofsteader was taking roll, Jason leaned over and whispered conspiratorially, "Have you talked to Petey yet about David?"

"A little," Val whispered back, "after the movie yesterday morning." She swallowed. She still wasn't used to talking to Jason like this. It made her mouth a little dry.

"And?"

Val shook her head. "No dice," she said. "She thinks he's okay where animals are concerned."

"Animals?" Jason asked. Mr. Hofsteader looked in their direction with a frown, and Jason added hurriedly, "Never mind. I've got an idea about how we can get them together so she can see what a really terrific guy he is."

Val sat up straight. Then, from the other side, Petey asked, "How's it going?"

"What do you mean, how's it going?" Val responded, even though she knew very well what Petey was asking.

Petey made a face at her. "With Jason," she said. "Are you working on him?"

"Uh-huh," Val said. "But no luck so far."

Petey looked dejected. "I'll keep my fingers crossed," she said.

Mr. Hofsteader put down his roll. "I see that some of you are very anxious to begin this morning's lesson," he said pleasantly. "Valerie Cassidy, why don't you close your book and tell us what you've discovered from your reading about the Shakers and their influence on American society?"

With a sigh of relief, Val began to recite. Luckily, Mr. Hofsteader had asked her about the one thing she had studied last night.

A few minutes before the bell was due to ring, while Mr. Hofsteader was handing out some homework, Val heard a hiss and then felt something hit her arm.

"*Psst*—Val!" It was Jason. He pointed down at the floor beside her, where a tiny folded triangle of white notebook paper lay. Petey saw Jason's gesture and her eyes sparkled with a hopeful look.

"Hey," she whispered, "it's a note! Jason's sending you a note!"

Mr. Hofsteader's back was turned. Swiftly, Val bent over and picked up the note and unfolded it. "My idea," the note said, "is to get Petey and David together, like a date. Can you bring Petey to the Bear's Lair after school today? David and I will meet you there." There was a heart drawn at the bottom of the note.

Val turned to Jason, nodding. "I think so," she mouthed.

"Let *me* see it," Petey reached for the slip of paper. "What does he say?"

Panic-stricken, Val crumpled the note. She couldn't let Petey see it, not with that heart drawn on the bottom! "He . . . he says," she stammered, "that we should meet him this afternoon. At the Lair. Can you come?" While she was talking, she shoved the paper into her notebook.

"*Can* I?" Petey said ecstatically, clasping her hands together. "Just try to keep me away! Oh, Val, you're *terrific*!"

"A-hem," Mr. Hofsteader's deep bass boomed behind them, so loudly that Val jumped. "I think," he said, his voice heavy with sarcasm, "that is enough." He handed Petey a paper. "And if you want my opinion, Alberta, I think your time would be better spent studying than whispering—at least until your grades improve."

Petey blushed. "Yes, sir," she said. "You're right, Mr. Hofsteader."

Mr. Hofsteader smiled icily. "And to make sure that you *do* program some time into your busy schedule for studying, you can do thirty minutes' detention this afternoon." He turned to Val. "And you can join her, Valerie." He looked down at the notebook, where Jason's paper was sticking out. "I'm sure you're aware of the rule against passing notes, aren't you?"

Val nodded, her face flaming, and Mr. Hofsteader turned to walk back to his desk.

"Excuse me, sir," Jason said, straightening his shoulders. "That was *my* note. Val wasn't responsible for it."

Val gave him a grateful look. It probably wouldn't change Mr. Hofsteader's mind, but it was nice to know that Jason wanted to stand up for her.

"I appreciate your candor, Jason," Mr. Hofsteader said without turning around. "Thirty minutes for you, too." At that moment the bell rang.

"Well," Petey said philosophically as she and Val walked down the hall together, "at least we all have detention. Then afterward, we can go to the Lair."

"David, too," Val said, dodging out of the way of a couple of boys who were racing down the hall, tossing a basketball back and forth.

Petey raised her eyebrows. "David?" She grinned. "It sounds like you might be weakening just a little."

"Not on your life," Val said. She stopped in front of her locker and began to fiddle with the lock. "But Jason wants to bring him. Any objections?"

"No." Petey leaned against the row of lockers. "But how are we going to get home? We're obviously going to miss the bus."

"I'll call my dad," Val said, collecting her math book. "He'll give us a ride, if we don't mind hanging around his office until six or so."

Petey smiled dreamily. "Mind? I'd hang around until *midnight* if it meant spending time with Jason. I mean, even detention will be a dream." She grabbed Val's arm and squeezed it happily. "Val, you're a miracle worker! How'd you manage it?"

"It was easy," Val muttered. She felt like a jerk—an absolute and total jerk!

The Bear's Lair, the local after-school hangout, was crowded by the time Val, Petey, and Jason got there. David had already saved them a table in the corner, under the row of photographs of all the past football and basketball teams. A red-and-white letter sweater was hung on another wall, along with a cluster of cheerleaders' pompoms and a big red A.

"Hi," David said, pulling out a chair. Val stared at him. He seemed different somehow, definitely nicer-looking. Then she realized it was because he wasn't wearing his glasses.

"What happened to your glasses?" Petey asked, sitting in the chair David held for her.

"I got contacts," David explained. "My mom

got tired of buying me new glasses every time I broke my old ones."

"Oh," Petey said. She turned to Jason. "That was really nice of you this morning," she said softly, "to take the blame for passing the note to Val." She put her elbows on the table and gazed soulfully at Jason.

Jason shrugged. "No big deal," he muttered, shifting uncomfortably. The waitress came and took their orders for soft drinks. When she had gone, he turned to David. "Listen," Jason said, "why don't you tell the girls about that terrific idea you had for a class project?"

"Oh," David said, "selling rubber stamps, you mean?" He leaned forward eagerly. "You know those little rubber gizmos that you stamp things with? Well, there's this place in town that makes them up to order. I was thinking that the class could maybe draw up a bunch of different things—you know, like the school mascot, caricatures of the teachers, stuff like that—and get the stamps made and then sell them to the other kids."

"Hey, that sounds great," Val said enthusiastically. "I bet they'd really sell fast. And it beats trying to sell those stupid boxes of greeting cards that we can only peddle to our grandmothers."

"Sounds good," Petey agreed halfheartedly.

She looked at Jason, turning her back on David. "How do you think *The Trip to Bountiful* is coming along? Do you think we'll be ready for next week's performance?"

Val sighed. No matter how nice David was, it wasn't going to be easy to turn Petey's attention away from Jason. At least David wasn't looking discouraged—in fact, there was a stubborn set to his mouth and he was leaning forward to get back into the conversation. Val was glad. David was too nice a guy to get hurt. When she caught Jason's eye he smiled a little and nodded, showing that he was on the same wavelength.

"I guess we'll be ready," Jason said, in answer to Petey's question. "What do you think, David? After all, you're in charge of the sets and the lighting. Do you think your crew is going to have everything finished and up by next Friday night?"

"It's looking good," David answered, "barring catastrophes." He turned to Petey and asked, "How are the costumes coming along?"

After half an hour or so of conversation, Jason looked at his watch. "Listen," he said, "I've got to split. I promised my mom I'd do a couple of errands for her, and it's getting late." He reached under the table and gave Val's hand a brief squeeze. "Let's do this again soon," he added, with a meaningful look at Val.

Petey didn't see the look. "Oh, yes," she said eagerly. "Let's!"

It was starting to snow again as Val and Petey walked the two blocks to Val's father's law office. Val's hands were in her pockets, her fingers still tingling from Jason's warm touch.

"Do you think we're getting anywhere?" Petey asked as they tramped through a snowdrift. She pulled her green beret more snugly down over her ears.

Val stuck out her tongue to catch a fat snowflake. "Maybe," she said cautiously. "It depends on where we're trying to get, I guess."

"Well," Petey said crisply, "I don't know about you, but *I'm* trying to get to the dance with Jason, remember? And I thought today took us one step closer. You know," she added, frowning thoughtfully, "I'm beginning to feel pretty comfortable around him. Maybe I should just take the direct approach. I could call him tonight and ask him." She sighed. "I mean, he can't do any worse than say no, can he?"

Val shivered. "Oh, I wouldn't do that," she said, knowing that she sounded strange. "At least, not just yet. I'd wait a few days and see what develops." She felt trapped, and changed the subject. "Hey, doesn't David look cuter now that he's got contacts instead of glasses?"

Petey nodded. "Definitely," she said, reflecting. They stopped to wait for the walk light. "You know, I never realized before how really *nice* he is. He's got a lot of clever ideas, too. I'll bet a lot of kids would go for those rubber stamps. They'd probably be a big hit."

Val felt a little bubble of hope. Maybe, just maybe, Jason's scheme was working. Maybe Petey *was* beginning to like David. But Petey's next words popped her bubble immediately.

"I just don't understand," she said crossly as the light changed and they stepped off the curb, "why you won't consider asking David to the dance."

Chapter Six

It was nearly nine o'clock and Val was just getting out of her bubble bath when she heard the phone ringing. Wilson answered it, and then he pounded on the bathroom door.

"It's for you, Val," he yelled.

"Tell whoever it is that I'm busy," Val called back as she reached for a towel. "I'm all wet."

"Well, okay, but it's a boy," Wilson persisted. "He says his name is Jason?"

Val swiped at herself with the towel, pulled on her terry-cloth robe, and made it to the telephone in three quick strides. "Hello?" she said breathlessly. She put her back against the wall and slid down it until she was sitting on the floor. "Sorry to keep you waiting."

"Hi." Jason's voice was deep and throaty, and it sent shivers through her. "How did we do with Operation David and Petey this afternoon?"

"We weren't exactly a smashing success, I'm afraid," Val said with a sigh. "Petey likes the way he looks in his new contacts, and she says that he's got terrific ideas. But she's got a better one."

"Oh yeah? What's that?"

Val couldn't help grinning. "She thinks I ought to ask David to the dance. That way the four of us could double-date."

"Uh-oh," Jason groaned. "Hey, we've got trouble."

"You know, Jason, this whole thing just doesn't feel right to me, somehow," Val said. "I mean, I keep worrying that I'm trying to force Petey to do something she doesn't want to do—just so I can get what *I* want." She twisted the telephone cord around her finger, hoping that Jason could understand what she was having such a hard time saying. "It makes me feel . . . well, sort of like a jerk," she confessed lamely. "If you know what I mean."

Jason chuckled sympathetically. "Yeah, I know," he said. "But you should have heard David after you two left this afternoon."

"What did he say?"

"He went on and on about how great Petey is and how he wishes they could get together.

You wouldn't feel like a jerk if you could hear *his* side of it. You'd feel like you were doing a terrific public service to get the two of them together. He's really stuck on her."

"Well, maybe," Val conceded. But she still wasn't convinced. She still felt awkward and confused and unhappy, which was really a shame, considering how wonderful it felt to hear Jason's voice and to know that he liked her.

"Anyway," Jason went on, "David's got this idea, and I wanted to check it out with you and make sure you thought it was okay."

Val giggled and pulled her bare feet up under her robe. "*Another* idea? Does it have anything to do with rubber stamps?"

"It's even better than rubber stamps," Jason said confidently. "You know the program we've been working on in computer class for the last couple of weeks—the one that matches people up?"

"Sure," Val said. The class had written most of the program together. They'd entered all their likes and dislikes into the computer and written a program that matched everybody up on the basis of their input. On the day after they ran the program in class to find out who was matched, the pairs were supposed to wear matching clothes, walk to class together, eat lunch together, and find out as much about each other as they could. "Aren't we supposed to run it in class Monday?" she asked. Computer class was seventh period.

"Right," Jason said. "Well, David wants to fix the program so that he and Petey are matched. That will give him the chance to spend the whole day with her on Tuesday. He figures that proximity ought to do the trick."

Val frowned doubtfully. "Fix the program? How do you do that?"

"Listen, it's a piece of cake. All we have to do is get the master disk and the data file and enter a few changes on the computer. Then when we run the program, it'll pair up David and Petey."

"You make it sound very simple," Val said, a little confused.

"It is." He sounded very pleased with himself. "It's so simple that it would take only a second to pair *us* up too, if you wanted to. How about it?"

"Whoa," Val said quickly. "That's going a little too far. Petey might suspect something if it happened that way." She hesitated. "Listen, Jason, what if Mr. Burns catches you fooling with the program? Or what if Petey finds out what you've done and refuses to go along with it?"

Jason sounded confident. "Don't worry,"

56

he said. "We won't get caught. And how could Petey find out—unless *you* tell her."

"I'm not going to tell Petey," Val said emphatically. "This is one secret that's better kept."

Jason's tone turned low and warm. "Listen, Val, just remember that we're doing this for us, huh? I mean, *you're* the one I want to be with."

"Me too," Val said. After he had hung up she stared at the phone for a long time. Then she put it down, very gently, and got to her feet, pulling her robe more tightly around her.

Wilson was standing in the doorway of his room, regarding her with a quizzical look on his face. "*What* aren't you going to tell Petey?" he demanded.

"Oh, nothing," Val said, heading back to the bathroom. "It's a secret." She stopped. Wilson was still watching her.

"I thought you and Petey didn't have secrets," he remarked. There was a little frown on his face and he looked anxious. "I thought best friends told each other all their secrets."

"We do," Val replied. "Except for this one." She went into the bathroom and shut the door and dried her hair. She was trying to remember the warm, rich sound of Jason's voice when he said "*You're* the one I want to be with."

But Wilson's voice kept interrupting. "I thought you and Petey didn't have any secrets," was the refrain that kept on playing over and over again in her head, like a stuck record.

On Monday morning, before homeroom period, Val was getting her books out of her locker when Jason skidded up beside her.

"Listen, Val," he said breathlessly. "David's not going to be here this afternoon. He has to go to the dentist. Something about his braces."

"Uh-oh," Val said. She closed her locker and turned, looking nervously over her shoulder for Petey. "Does that mean that the computer caper is off?"

"No way." Jason shook his head. "David gave me all the changes to put into the computer program. But this afternoon is our last shot at changing the program." He gave her a narrow look. "We've got to do it today or give up the idea."

"We?" Val asked apprehensively.

"Yeah," Jason said, falling into step beside her. "As in you and me. Look," he added hastily, "you don't actually have to do anything with the computer. I'll take care of that. All you have to do is stand guard."

"Stand guard!" Val exclaimed. This scheme was beginning to sound like a detective movie on television. It was scary.

"David says that the master disk and the data file are both in Mr. Burns's desk," Jason went on. "Burns is lunch monitor today, so he'll be busy both fifth and sixth periods. There'll be plenty of time to get the disks and make the changes, then test the new program and put the disks back before seventh-period class. Okay?"

Val nodded reluctantly. "Are you *sure* about this, Jason?" she asked. "I mean, you're sure we can make the changes in the program so that David and Petey get matched up?"

"Yeah, I'm sure about that part, at least," Jason said. He grinned. "What I'm not sure about is what happens afterward. I guess we just have to get them together and let nature take its course." He gave her an admiring look. "Hey, you look fantastic in that pink sweater."

Val was glad that she didn't have a test that morning, because she almost certainly would have failed it. She kept worrying about whether she and Jason would be caught taking the computer disk out of Mr. Burns's desk. She tried telling herself that it really wasn't a big deal. After all, they weren't going

59

to destroy it or steal it or anything like that. It was all a very innocent scheme.

But no matter how often she reassured herself, by fifth period she was feeling really apprehensive. She told Petey that she had some library research to do during lunch and walked hurriedly toward Mr. Burns's office.

"Looks like we're locked out," Jason said, grim-faced, gesturing toward the computer room next to Mr. Burns's office.

"Listen, Jason, maybe this isn't such a good idea after all. Maybe we should just—"

Jason shook his head. "I'm hoping that the key is in Mr. Burns's office," he said.

"Which might be locked," Val said.

Jason tried Mr. Burns's door. It wasn't locked. "You stand in the hallway," he said, "and give a whistle if anybody comes around the corner." He disappeared into the office and closed the door while Val leaned against the wall, trying to look nonchalant. A couple of minutes later, a boy rounded the corner and loped down the hall. Val tried to whistle but her mouth was too dry and all she could do was make a funny little hissing sound. The boy gave her a curious look and kept on going.

Another minute later, Jason came out of Mr. Burns's office, a key in one hand and two computer disks in the other.

"Voilà!" he said. "Now for step two." He opened the glass-windowed door to the computer room.

"Listen," Val said urgently, "we've got a problem."

Jason paused. "What is it?"

Val colored. "I can't whistle," she muttered. "I tried a minute ago, but nothing came out."

Jason laughed and touched her cheek lightly. "Well, okay then, why don't you just rap on the door. Okay?"

Val leaned against the wall. "Okay, I guess." She sucked in a nervous breath. "Good luck." She watched through the door as Jason sat down in front of one of the computers and turned it on. He began to type, and in a few seconds the screen was full of green numbers. He scrolled the numbers quickly until he found what he wanted, and then began to type again, looking down at a white card on the desk beside him.

Just at that moment, Val heard voices coming down the hall. It was Mrs. Robertson, the home ec teacher, and Mr. Paul, who taught shop, engrossed in conversation. Val tensed fearfully but they only looked up and nodded as they walked past. When they got to the intersection with the next hallway, still within sight, they stood talking with their backs to her.

Sharply, Val rapped on the door. *"Ps-ss-t,* Jason," she said, her voice strained. "There's a couple of teachers down at the end of the hall. Aren't you done yet?"

"Yeah, I'm done," Jason said, "but I haven't tested the program yet."

The conversation at the end of the hall grew louder and Val looked up. It was Mr. Burns! He was talking to the other teachers and his back was toward her, but he could turn and start down the hall at any minute. And if he did, they'd be discovered!

"It's Mr. Burns!" Val said, frantic. "We've got to go before he catches us! Come on, Jason!"

Jason pulled the disks from the computer and turned it off. In a moment he had closed and locked the computer room door and then slipped into Mr. Burns's office to return the disks. Then he was back out in the hallway again and they walked away quickly. Val looked back over her shoulder. Mr. Burns had started down the hall toward his office, walking jauntily with his hands in his pockets and whistling. He caught a glimpse of the two of them as they turned the corner and waved.

"Whew!" Val said. "That was close!" She sagged against a wall and giggled with relief.

"I was really scared there for a minute. I thought he was going to catch us!"

"Actually, we're not home free yet, Val," Jason said as he searched through his pockets.

Val stared at him. "What do you mean?"

"I didn't get a chance to test the program to see if it would run with the changes I made." They began to walk down the hall toward the library. "Every time you change a computer program, you run the risk of getting a bug in it. So you have to test it to make sure that there aren't any bugs."

Val bit her lip. "What will happen if there *is* a bug?" she asked worriedly.

"Then the program won't run. The screen will show errors."

"And then what happens?"

Jason shook his head. "I don't know. It depends. Maybe Mr. Burns will just make us fix whatever's wrong, without looking at the rest of the program. On the other hand, maybe he'll figure out that somebody was messing with it and . . ."

Val looked at him, horrified. "Oh, no, Jason, he *saw* us! Do you think he'll figure out that *we* were the ones who were fooling with it?"

Jason gave her a reassuring grin and reached for her hand. "Hey, let's not freak out, okay? Just remember that we were doing a good deed for a couple of friends—not stealing the crown jewels. If Mr. Burns does figure it out, I'll tell him what I was doing. It's no big deal."

Val tried to smile. "Okay," she said. It felt very good to be walking down the hall holding Jason's hand. But she couldn't help glancing over her shoulder. What if Petey saw them?

"Just the same," Jason said, giving her hand a squeeze and dropping it, "keep your fingers crossed that the program works. And that Mr. Burns doesn't find that white card."

"The white card?" Val paused at the door to the library, her heart thudding wildly.

"Yeah. The one with David's instructions on it." Jason looked a little sheepish. "I've looked in all my pockets and I can't find it. I guess I left it in the computer room."

Chapter Seven

Thank heavens, Val thought as she walked into the computer room at the beginning of sixth period, that she didn't have to wait a whole day to find out whether the program was going to run. As it was, she'd spent the rest of fifth period hunched over a book in the library, biting her nails and trying not to think of what would happen if Mr. Burns figured out that the computer program had been doctored.

From across the room, Jason waved a white index card at her and grinned triumphantly. Val let out a relieved breath. Well, at least they hadn't left behind any evidence.

Val went over and sat down with Petey and Ashley Taft, one of the other girls in class.

"Missed you at lunch," Petey said. "Did you get your research done?"

Val made a wry face. "Well, not done, exactly," she said truthfully. "But I worked at it."

Ashley looked up from some notes she was scribbling. "Hi, Val," she said. She pushed her long auburn hair back over her shoulders and adjusted her gold-rimmed glasses. "Say, do you have any juicy items for the column? Tomorrow's my deadline."

"Sorry," Val said. "I can't think of a thing." Ashley wrote the gossip column for the *Reporter*, the school newspaper. The column, which she called "Tidbits," was the first thing everybody read when the paper came out.

"Me either," Petey said. She sighed wistfully. "I mean, I *wish* I had an item, but I don't. Not yet, anyway."

Ashley leaned forward, her gray eyes eagerly intent behind her glasses. She had a reputation for digging out gossip; some of the kids even said that her nose twitched when she got wind of a possible romantic involvement. "Can you give me a little more detail?" she asked. "I mean, who's involved?"

Val was glad that Petey didn't have time to answer. Mr. Burns came into the room, carrying the computer disks. "Okay, gang," he said. "This is the moment of truth. Today's the day when we find out whether our computer program works with our data file—and when *you* discover the identity of your secret soul mate."

A wave of giggles washed over the room as Mr. Burns went over to a computer and slipped one of the disks into the drive. "Everybody hold your breath," he said. "Let's hope this thing works."

Ashley stood up. "I'm going to watch," she said, and went over to stand beside the computer. "I guess if I run short on items I can always put something about soul mates into the column."

Val pulled a strand of hair forward and began to chew on it nervously. She felt as if a whole flock of butterflies were doing figure eights inside her. Was the program going to work?

Petey suddenly snapped her fingers. "Hey, maybe the program will pair Jason and me!" Then she slumped down in her chair. "No," she sighed, "we don't have anything in common. Except the drama club, that is."

Val looked at her questioningly. "If you don't have anything in common," she asked, "why do you want to go out with him?"

Petey wrinkled her nose. "Because he's so *cute*," she said. "And he's popular and into everything and—" She shrugged. "What other reasons do you want? I mean, isn't that enough?"

Val sat back, thinking. When you got right down to it, she didn't seem to have very much in common with Jason either, at least, that she knew about. Maybe if there was the right kind of physical chemistry, you were attracted to the other person first and then found out later that you had things in common. She glanced at Petey. Or maybe, with some people, it worked the other way. You found out you had things in common and *then* you discovered an attraction. Maybe it would be that way with Petey and David.

Mr. Burns leaned over the computer and turned on the printer. Jason was right behind him and he winked at Val.

"Hey, look at that!" Mr. Burns said as the printer clicked rapidly and the paper began to feed into a stack. "Our program is a success! Congratulations, everybody! Good work!"

Val let out her breath in an explosive sigh of relief. Everybody clapped. The printer stopped clicking and Mr. Burns ripped off the pages and held them up as he looked around the room.

"Don't forget, gang, that tomorrow is the day that all the soul mates wear matching outfits. I expect you to spend as much time as possible together and find out as much as you can about each another. Focus especially on what you have in common, and try to find out why the computer matched you up. Then use the word processor to write a two-hundred-word report on what you found—papers are due in exactly one week. Everybody understand the assignment?"

There was a chorus of enthusiastic yeses.

"Well, this is the moment you've all been waiting for." Mr. Burns handed the pages to Ashley. "Ashley, suppose you read the names of our secret soul mates."

Ashley cleared her throat and pushed her glasses up on her nose, looking important. Val listened anxiously. The program had worked, but had it done what it was supposed to do? Had it paired up Petey and David? Jason's name was close to the top of the list; he was paired with another guy, somebody that Val didn't know very well. The next name she heard was her own—she was paired with, of all people, Ashley Taft!

Petey leaned over and rolled her eyes. "*Ashley* is your secret soul mate?"

Val shrugged and laughed. "What can I say?" she asked. "There must be something about both of us that doesn't meet the eye." Privately, she was disappointed. She'd hoped she would be paired with Jason. And she couldn't think of one thing she and Ashley had in common.

"Alberta Boyd . . ." Ashley read. She paused

and looked over the top of her glasses with a smile.

"Hey, that's me," Petey said. She cocked her head, listening.

". . . is the secret soul mate of David MacIntosh," Ashley concluded.

"Oh, peaches," Petey muttered, half under her breath.

Ashley glanced at Mr. Burns. "David? I guess he's not here today."

"He had to go out of town," Jason volunteered. "He'll be back tomorrow."

"Why don't you call him tonight and tell him about the match," Mr. Burns suggested to Petey. "That way you can decide what you're going to wear, and start planning your papers."

Petey sighed. "Yeah, I guess so," she said.

Jason and Val shared a secret smile. It was a success! Their scheme had worked—so far, anyway.

But Petey was frowning. "David MacIntosh?" she said to Val, with a puzzled shake of her head. "You know, I think this computer program is absolutely one hundred percent wacko. I mean, you and Ashley Taft? Me and David MacIntosh? What in the world do I have in common with David?" She paused, looking thoughtful. "Except for liking animals, that is. Do you think maybe that was what got us together?"

Val smiled and patted Petey on the arm. "Just wait until tomorrow," she said happily. "I'm sure that you'll find out."

The next morning, when Val got on the school bus, she found David and Petey sitting together. They both wore very silly grins, Val noticed.

"Okay," she said, "let's see your outfits."

Petey stood up and pulled open her coat, revealing a pair of denim overalls over a red sweat shirt. A blue bandana was knotted around her neck. "What do you think?" she asked.

"Hey," Val said approvingly as Petey plopped back down beside David, "pretty cute." She looked at David. "You too?" she asked.

He nodded happily. "We've got hats, too," he added, holding up two old-fashioned engineer's caps. "And matching boots." He nudged Petey, who stuck her foot out into the aisle. She was wearing a pair of red knee-high rubber boots.

"Just in case we get stuck in a snowdrift," Petey said. "What are you and Ashley wearing?"

"Nothing very spectacular." Val opened her coat to display the jeans and red-and-white school T-shirts she and Ashley had finally decided on over the phone the night before. "We had a hard time agreeing," she said with

71

a shrug. "So much for common ideas." She glanced at David. "Were you surprised to find out that you and Petey were soul mates?" she asked.

David gave her a meaningful grin. "Not as surprised as Petey was," he replied. Val looked at him, then looked again. There was something else different about him. What was it? His braces were gone. And without them, even in that funny getup, David was positively good-looking.

"Yeah," Petey said dryly. "You bet I was surprised." With a look of determination, she pulled out her notebook. "Come on, David. We've got to figure out why the stupid computer thought we were soul mates. I blew Burns's last test because I didn't have time to study, and I intend to get an A on this paper or die in the attempt."

Val sat back and stared out the window, nibbling on her lower lip. The scheme just had to work!

When the bus got to school, Ashley, wearing jeans and the school T-shirt, was waiting for Val at her locker, and she looked harried.

"Listen, Val, I don't have a lot of time for this project today," she said apologetically. "Would you mind if I just put in an appearance with you at class and we do the stuff for our papers later? 'Tidbits' is due today, and

I'm still short two or three items. I absolutely *have* to get it finished before noon or I'm really sunk. The paper's coming out tomorrow."

"Sure, that's okay," Val said, relieved that she didn't have to spend a lot of time with Ashley. They really *didn't* have a lot in common. Maybe when Jason had changed the computer program to match up David and Petey, he'd messed up the other matches. It was something she'd have to ask him about.

Val cradled her books and they began to walk toward the stairs. On the stairs up ahead, Petey and David were on their way to homeroom, their heads together, talking and laughing. Funny thing—she'd always thought David was shy and studious. But in those overalls, without his glasses, he didn't look studious at all, or shy. He looked as if he was having fun.

Beside her, Ashley craned her neck, looking up the stairs. "*That's* interesting," she said musingly.

Val turned toward her. "What's interesting?"

"Those two." Ashley gestured toward Petey and David. The pair had reached the top of the stairs, where Petey's homeroom was, and Petey was leaning against the wall. David was standing beside her, looking down at her, utterly absorbed in what she was saying. "Would you say," Ashley added, "that David is looking at Petey as if he's got a crush on her, or what?"

An alarm bell went off inside Val's head. Ashley was notorious for using 'Tidbits' to start rumors. If she mentioned in her column that David and Petey were involved, when the paper came out tomorrow *everybody* would be talking about it.

"You're Petey's best friend," Ashley continued, taking a steno notebook out of her purse. "What can you tell me about this interesting new relationship?"

"It's *not* a new relationship," Val tried to explain. "It's—"

"Oh, I see." Ashley began to scribble. "So they've been keeping their longtime involvement a secret." She looked up. "Why were they keeping it a secret? Was there somebody else? Were their parents upset about them seeing each other?"

"For Pete's sake, that's not it at *all*," Val exclaimed. "Look, Ashley, there's really *no* relationship. The computer . . ." She swallowed, thinking about what she and Jason had done yesterday. They'd been responsible for this whole thing. "The computer just matched them up, that's all," she said lamely.

"Computers don't lie," Ashley insisted. She studied Val, her eyes narrowed slightly, her pencil poised over her notebook page. "So this relationship has been going on—under wraps, so to speak—for several months. I suppose, though, now that the computer has brought their involvement out into the open, that Petey will ask him to the Valentine's Day dance."

"No, of course she won't," Val said, shaking her head emphatically. "Petey isn't interested in—"

She stopped. She and Jason had gone to a lot of trouble to set up this match, hoping that Petey would discover she liked David and ask him to the dance, leaving Val and Jason free to go together. Now, here was gossipy Ashley Taft, offering her column in the school paper as another means of achieving the same end. So what was wrong with giving the idea just one more little boost?

Ashley was waiting, watching Val with avid curiosity. "She isn't interested in what?" she prompted.

Val grinned. "There's no use in trying to cover it up."

Ashley began to scribble energetically. "So, Petey *is* definitely interested in David MacIntosh, and she'll probably ask him to the dance?"

"Yes," Val answered, deciding to help move the relationship along. "I suppose you could say that, if you wanted to. You could say that

Petey's interested in David. And I suppose you might even stick in that part about the dance, if you wanted to."

Ashley closed her notebook as the bell rang. "Don't worry, Val," she said, patting Val on the arm. "I won't put your name in print. You'll be that very famous person, Anonymous Source."

"Thanks," Val said as Ashley turned to hurry away. "I think," she added, under her breath.

Chapter Eight

Val hesitated for a long time before she dialed Jason's number that evening. She hadn't called him before, and she felt awkward, but her uneasiness faded away when she heard the warmth in his voice as he said hello.

"Hey," he said, "David told me that he and Petey had a super day."

"They did?" Val asked. "That's great." Petey had had play practice after school, and Val hadn't talked to her that evening.

"Yeah. According to David, they discovered all sorts of things they have in common." Jason chuckled. "Birds and snakes and—"

"Snakes?"

"David collects them. He's got this terrific boa constrictor named Balboa that he feeds baby mice."

"Yuck!" She shuddered. "I've known Petey

77

forever and she's never said anything about a secret love of snakes."

"Well, actually," Jason said, "what they have in common is that they're both planning to be famous veterinarians someday."

"They may not have to wait that long," Val said nervously. "They may be famous tomorrow."

"Oh, yeah?" Jason sounded interested. "How come?"

Val told him about Ashley's gossip column. "I didn't actually come right out and *tell* her that Petey was going to ask David to the dance," she said, concluding her story. "I just sort of hinted, and you know Ashley, she took it from there." She sighed guiltily. "I'm afraid I've gone too far. Who knows what Ashley's going to put in the column. I only know that everybody is going to read it."

Jason was silent for a minute. Then he said, "You know that the kids who read Ashley's column take it with a grain of salt. And David will probably be thrilled to read something about him and Petey."

"I know," Val said. "But what about Petey? If she thinks I had anything to do with the article, she's going to be boiling mad at me."

They talked for a few more minutes, then said good-night. But an hour later, when Val went to bed, she was still thinking about what she had done. Was it right? Was Petey going to be hurt? But whether it was right or wrong, it was too late now to do anything about it. When she finally fell asleep, she dreamed that she and Petey had gone to the dance together, dressed in overalls and red sweat shirts, and that Ashley Taft was there too, dressed like a witch and carrying her own portable computer.

Early the next morning, Petey phoned and asked Val if she wanted a ride to school. Twenty minutes later, her mother drove up the snowy drive, and Val climbed in the car.

Petey twisted around and put her chin on her arms on the back of the front seat. "So how did it go with Ashley yesterday?" she asked.

Val grimaced, thinking about the gossip column. "Don't ask," she replied, loosening her muffler. "How was it with David? Did you get enough for your paper?"

"Oh, yeah!" Petey said enthusiastically. "I mean, the computer was right on when it matched the two of us!"

Val couldn't help smiling. "You mean, you and David turned out to have lots in common?" she asked. At least the computer match hadn't been a total and utter disaster—the way Ashley's gossip column threatened to be.

If only there were a way to keep Petey from reading the paper!

"Yeah, we did, as a matter of fact." Petey grinned. "You know, he's going to be a vet, like me."

"Hmm," Val said. She gave Petey a quick glance. "Do I detect a slight interest here?"

"Listen," Petey said, changing the subject, "we've *got* to finish cutting out those dumb hearts and cupids for the dance. Maybe we'd better do it tonight. Tomorrow night is dress rehearsal for *The Trip to Bountiful*, and the play is Friday."

"Okay," Val agreed. "Why don't you come over after dinner and we'll do it at my house?"

By the time they got to school, there was a stack of school newspapers beside the front door. Val walked past it quickly, hoping that Petey wouldn't see it, but Petey stopped and picked up two copies. "Hey, don't forget your *Reporter*," she said, handing one to Val.

"There's probably nothing much in it," Val muttered, snatching it from Petey and stuffing it into her notebook without glancing at it. "It's usually nothing but ancient history—basketball games that we played two weeks ago, stuff like that." Suddenly Val had an idea. "Listen, Petey, why don't we boycott the paper? We could stop reading it until they promise to print something that happened before the turn of the century."

Petey stopped at her locker. "Oh, the paper's not so bad," she remarked, "considering the fact that nothing very interesting ever happens around here. And anyway, it's our *duty* as students to read it. If you want to read the latest news, you ought to read Ashley Taft's column. She's always got the scoops."

"Yeah," Val muttered, "but whether her scoops are true or not is anybody's guess."

Just then two girls walked by, their arms full of books. "So it's all out in the open, huh, Petey?" one of them teased. "Hey, what were you waiting for?"

"She was waiting for him to get rid of his glasses and his braces, of course," the other one said with a giggle. "Now that he's changed from a frog to a prince, she doesn't care who knows."

Petey looked from one to the other, puzzled. "What's that supposed to mean?" she asked. She looked at Val. "Do *you* know what they're talking about?"

Val shrugged and shook her head, hoping desperately that her guilt didn't show on her face. "I don't have the slightest," she said.

Petey turned back to her locker. "You guys are crazy," she said emphatically.

Both girls giggled as they continued down

the hall. "You'd better read Ashley's column," one of them called over her shoulder.

"Read Ashley's column?" Petey asked. She put her books down on the floor and began to leaf through the paper. "Here it is." As she began to read, she gasped and her eyes widened. "Oh, my gosh," she muttered.

Petey read out loud, rapidly.

"Everybody's buzzing about the discovery of the longtime secret relationship between Petey Boyd and David MacIntosh. It seems that the *computer* picked them out as soul mates, revealing their hidden attraction for each other. A certain anonymous source says that Petey is planning to ask David to the Valentine's Day dance. Sounds like a romantic fairy tale, doesn't it? You'll probably think so, especially when you see the way love has transformed David. He's shed his glasses and his braces, and he looks like a prince. Good luck, Petey and David!"

Petey lowered the paper and looked at Val, horror-struck. "Oh, wow," she moaned. "Longtime secret relationship? Romantic fairy tale? Oh, wow."

"Oh, Petey, I'm so *sorry*!" Val exclaimed.

"Sorry? Why should *you* be sorry?" Petey

wadded up the paper and threw it on the floor. "It's that stupid Ashley Taft!" she exclaimed angrily. "She ran out of gossip and she's *inventing* stuff—just inventing it, out of nothing." She turned back to the locker and hid her face behind the door. "What's David going to say when he reads this?" she moaned.

"Well," Val said, trying to calm her friend, "he'll probably think it's okay. Ashley says he looks like a prince."

"Yeah, but she says he's in *love!*" Petey banged her fist on the locker. "How stupid!"

Val looked at her. "Are you sure it's stupid?" she asked quietly.

"*Sure,* I'm sure," Petey retorted. "I mean, David's got his snakes. He's not interested in girls."

"Maybe, maybe not," Val said. "He sure looked interested in you yesterday. And after all, he did go out of his way to sit by you in the movie the other morning." It was something she didn't feel guilty about saying. It was the *truth.*

Petey looked away. "Do you think that's where Ashley got the idea for this? From seeing us together yesterday, I mean?"

Val bit her lip. "I don't know," she said. "Probably."

Petey slammed her locker shut and picked

up her books. "Well," she said, squaring her shoulders, "I guess I'd better get ready to face up to it. There's probably going to be a lot of teasing today."

Val shook her head. "I'm sorry, Petey," she said again. "Really sorry."

"Ashley's the one who's going to be sorry," Petey threatened. "Just wait until I get my hands on her."

Chapter Nine

That evening, Val and her mother had just finished loading the dishwasher when they heard a car in the driveway. "That's probably Petey," Val said, going to the door and turning on the porch light. Outside, the snow was coming down in gusty spurts. But the car parked in the drive wasn't the Boyds' car. And the person stamping snow off his shoes, his breath frosty in the air, wasn't Petey. It was Jason!

For a moment, Val could hardly believe her eyes. She finally opened the door to let him in, her heart thumping. He was carrying something wrapped in green paper.

"I know I should have called," Jason said, pulling off his gloves. "But I had to go to the supermarket for my mom, and when I was there I saw this and I thought about you," he said, handing her the green package.

Val opened it and saw that it was a daffodil, a delicate golden daffodil, messenger of spring and bright sunshine. There was a little card with it that said "For Val."

"It kind of reminded me of your bright yellow sweater," he added with a grin.

She'd never gotten a flower from a boy before—and such a beautiful spring flower, on such a wintery night! "Thank you. It's beautiful!" she exclaimed. "Come inside while I find something to put it in."

They went into the kitchen and Jason perched on the kitchen stool at the counter while Val found a bud vase and put the daffodil in it. She glanced nervously up at the clock.

"I'd ask you to take off your coat and stay awhile," she said apprehensively, "but I'm expecting Petey in about ten minutes. We're making decorations for the dance."

Jason nodded. "Oh, yeah, the dance," he said. "How did it go with Petey today? Was she mad at you about the item in 'Tidbits'?"

"No, not at me," Val said, "although I'm sure she would have been if she'd known that I was the anonymous source. But she was really furious at Ashley. And everybody was teasing her." She looked at Jason. "How did David take it? Was he upset?"

Jason chuckled. "He didn't seem to be. He

didn't say so, but I have the feeling that he sort of liked that stuff about being a prince." A look of wry amusement came into his deep green eyes. "Actually, I came over to tell you something—something kind of funny."

Val sat down on the other stool. "Whatever it is," she said, "funny or not, I hope it doesn't make things more complicated than they already are."

Jason put his hand over hers on the counter. "You know the changes we made in the computer program? Well, this afternoon David and I were in the computer lab looking over the *old* program, the way it was before we doctored it. And we discovered something."

Val looked down at their hands. His fingers laced with hers were cold, but they felt strong and good. "What did you discover?" she asked.

"That we didn't have to alter the program after all."

"You mean," Val asked unbelievingly, "that Petey and David would have been matched *anyway*, even if we hadn't done all that cloak-and-dagger stuff?"

Jason nodded, grinning. "They were a pair from the very beginning. But the really funny part is that when we changed the program, we changed everybody else's match. The computer matched us all randomly, instead of pairing us according to our common interests."

"Oh," Val exclaimed. "So *that's* how I got stuck with Ashley Taft! I *knew* we didn't have anything in common." She shook her head, laughing. "What a mess! What do you think we ought to do?"

"Just leave things the way they are, and hope that Mr. Burns doesn't figure it out." He laughed. "Anyway, I think our prime objective is being accomplished. David says that he might even get up his nerve to ask Petey to the dance. Do you think she'd say yes?"

Val shrugged. "I don't know," she said. "She likes him, but—"

"Well, I'm getting kind of impatient, if you want to know the truth, Val," Jason said, his gaze intent on hers. "I mean, I'd like to spend more time with you at school, and we can't because of Petey." He leaned forward.

Val realized that Jason's lips were only inches away. Suddenly a feeling of panic filled her. He was going to kiss her! What should she do? She *wanted* to kiss him too, but was it right when they hadn't gotten things straightened out yet? And what if Petey walked in on them? What if—

There was a giggle from the hallway, and Jason pulled back. It was Wilson, crouched just outside the door. He had both hands over his mouth, and his shoulders were shaking with merriment.

"Wilson," Val said in a warning voice. Her face turned bright red. She got down off the stool and ran over to her brother and grabbed his shoulders. "Wilson Cassidy, why were you spying on me?"

"But I wasn't spying!" Wilson protested, still giggling. "I was just coming to the kitchen to get a drink, and I saw—"

Out in the drive a car door slammed. "It's Petey!" Val exclaimed frantically.

Jason laughed. "Okay if I use your kitchen door?" he asked. He gave her a quick wave, and then he was gone, out into the snow.

"Who was that guy?" Wilson asked curiously. "Is he your boyfriend? Were you going to let him kiss you, just like on TV?"

Val ignored him and went to the front door. Petey was knocking the snow off her shoes on the front porch. She came into the house, carrying a big paper bag, just as Jason stepped around the side, got into his car, and drove off.

"Hi," she said, coming in. "Who was that?" She glanced back over her shoulder as Val shut the door.

"Who was who?" Val asked.

"The person who just drove away, that's who," Petey said, shrugging out of her coat.

"Oh, just some friend of the family," Val said evasively.

Wilson came up behind her. "It was Val's boyfriend," he told Petey with a wildly gleeful chortle. "You should have *seen* it, Petey! He tried to ki—"

Val whirled swiftly and put her hand over Wilson's mouth. "Wilson," she said, "it's time for bed." And she hurried him, protesting, into the family room, where she turned him firmly over to her mother.

"What was Wilson trying to say?" Petey asked when Val came back into the hall, trying to compose herself. "What's this about a boyfriend? Have you been keeping something from me?" she asked with a wide grin.

Val felt her cheeks grow warm. "Oh, it's nothing," Val replied, not meeting Petey's curious glance. "You know little kids—sometimes their imaginations go into overdrive." She went to the refrigerator and got out a carton of milk. "Hey, how about some hot chocolate?"

Petey took the stool that Jason had just vacated. "Sounds good," she said, rubbing her hands. "It's cold and yucky out there." She saw the daffodil on the counter, a bright splash of yellow in the green glass vase. "Hey, what a pretty flower." She reached out and gently touched a delicate yellow petal. "Where did it come from?"

Val spilled a blob of chocolate on the counter. "Where did what come from?" she asked, stalling for time.

"This daffodil." Petey pointed. "The one right here on the counter."

"Oh." Val put the pan of chocolate milk on the stove and turned on the heat, not looking up. "It came from the supermarket, I guess."

"No, I mean, who *gave* it to you?" Petey picked up the card and waved it. "The card says 'For Val.' "

"For me?" Val stirred the chocolate furiously, trying to think of an explanation that wouldn't exactly be a lie. "Oh, yeah," she said finally. "Oh, well, Mom was shopping and . . ."

Mrs. Cassidy came into the kitchen. "Oh, hi, Petey," she said, with a bright smile. "I understand you girls are cutting out hearts tonight."

Hurriedly, Val poured the hot chocolate into cups. "Come on, Petey," she said, picking up the cups and heading for the door, before Petey could ask any more questions about the flower. "Let's go upstairs. We've got a lot of work to do."

"That's a lovely daffodil, Mrs. Cassidy," Petey said, sliding off the stool and following Val. "It makes me think of spring."

"Yes, doesn't it?" Mrs. Cassidy said. Val turned around as she left the room. Her mother was standing there, staring at the daffodil with a puzzled look.

"It makes me think of romance, too," Petey said as the two girls entered Val's room.

Val sat down on the bed and sipped her hot chocolate. "Speaking of romance," she began as nonchalantly as she could, "what's happening with you and David?"

"Not you, too?" Petey asked. "I thought you were my friend."

"I am," Val said. "That's why I asked." She managed a grin. "There seemed to be a lot of positive reaction to Ashley's item. I heard several kids in school today say what a cute couple you two are."

Petey frowned. "More to the point, I'd like to know what's happening with me and Jason? What have you been able to find out?"

"I asked first," Val said quickly.

"Yeah, well, what's happening with me and David is strictly *friendship,* no matter what Ashley Taft claims." Petey sipped her hot chocolate. "I mean, he's a *very* sweet guy, and I really like talking to him, but there's no spark. There's no romance." She looked up at Val and heaved a dramatic sigh. "There are no yellow daffodils, if you know what I mean."

Val looked away, feeling a sharp twinge of guilt when she thought of the yellow daffodil downstairs. "Even though he doesn't wear glasses and braces anymore?" she asked tentatively. "I mean, everybody's talking about how good-looking he really is. And he obviously likes you a lot. It shows in the way he looks at you."

"Yeah, I guess he does," Petey said slowly. "And to tell the truth, that's given me a lot to think about. I mean, Jason is obviously playing hard to get, and there is David, available and cute and very sweet." She grinned crookedly. "You know that old saying about a bird in the hand being worth two in the bush?"

Val laughed a little, suddenly feeling hopeful. "You mean," she said, looking at Petey thoughtfully, "that it might be better to ask somebody to the dance who's bound to say yes than somebody who might say no."

Petey nodded. "I was thinking along those lines, yes. But you really shouldn't be practical about romance."

Val sucked in her breath. "You shouldn't?"

"No, silly," Petey said, as if she had given the matter a great deal of thought. "About romance, you should be *romantic*. Your heart ought to go thud-thud-thud and your knees ought to feel weak when you're around the right guy. You ought to think rainbows and yellow daffodils all day long. Do you know what I mean?"

"Do I?" Val muttered under her breath thinking of the way she felt when she and Jason were together. Aloud, she said, "Yes, I guess I do. But maybe that's kind of unrealistic. I mean, your heart can't be pounding every minute you're with a guy, can it?"

"Well, my heart doesn't go thud-thud-thud and my knees don't feel weak when I'm around David—at all," Petey said, finishing the last of her hot chocolate. "We have plenty to talk about, and we have a lot of fun together. But the way I feel about him is that we could have a really great friendship, not a romance."

"Yeah, I guess I understand how you feel," Val said. She felt a surge of hopelessness. She was sick and tired of scheming and going behind Petey's back and feeling miserable about it. And anyway, no matter how hard she and Jason had tried, none of their schemes had worked. Maybe it was time to give up.

Petey tossed a pair of scissors to Val. "Well, now that we've got that straight," she said, "it's your turn." She began to cut out a paper heart. "What's happening with Jason?" she asked. "What do you think I ought to do about the dance?"

"Well, I think," Val said resignedly, "that you ought to ask him." She picked up a piece of construction paper and began to cut.

"You *do*?" Petey asked, sitting straight up, her blue eyes widening. "You mean, Jason has finally said that he'll say yes if I ask him?"

"Well, no," Val admitted lamely. "But it's beginning to seem kind of silly for you to keep putting it off. If you want to go to the dance with him, I think you should just march up to him and ask him."

"The problem is," Petey responded, "that my head says march and my knees say no. I really am a chicken." She put down her scissors "On the other hand, I guess maybe it really isn't fair to put you in the middle. I mean, I ought to be mature enough to do my own asking." She sighed. "This thing is *so* complicated."

Val didn't answer. What she wanted most of all was to confess the whole truth. She was going to have to tell her someday, anyway. Maybe now was the best time.

But just as Val was about to begin, the door burst open and Wilson came bouncing in, wearing his pajamas. He threw his arms around Val's neck and gave her a big, slurpy kiss on her cheek. "Good night, Val," he said. "Good night, Petey." He turned to Val. "Hey, Val, did you tell Petey about what happened in the kit—"

Hurriedly, Val got to her feet and grabbed Wilson's hand. "Bedtime, Willie," she said. "Come on." And she took him to his room.

When she came back Petey was tracing cupids on pink paper. "I've decided," she said, looking up.

"Decided what?"

"Decided what to do about Jason." She

paused, counting cupids. "Gosh, Val, these ridiculous cupids are going to take a *year* to cut out. We've got to do ten sheets of them."

Val sighed and took the sheet Petey had just finished tracing. "What did you decide?" she asked.

"I'm going to do it. I'm going to ask him."

Val's heart sank down and down, all the way to her toes, it seemed. "You are?"

"Yeah, I am. I'm tired of being a chicken. I'm going to ask him—on Friday."

"On Friday?" Val looked up. "But today's only Wednesday. Why are you putting it off?"

Petey sighed. "Because tomorrow night is dress rehearsal for the play," she said. "Which means that he'll have lots on his mind. He'll be able to think a lot more clearly on Friday." She picked up another piece of paper. "Anyway," she said, "I have to get used to not being a chicken. And that's going to take at least a day."

Chapter Ten

After Petey had left, Val sat on the floor in the upstairs hall and dialed Jason's number. When he answered she said, "I've decided it's time to stop scheming."

There was a silence on the other end of the line. Then Jason said in a disappointed voice, "After all that time they spent getting to know each other, she doesn't *like* David? He's such a great guy."

"Oh, she really likes him," Val said quickly. "The thing is that she doesn't feel *romantic* about him. She says you ought to feel romantic about the guy you go out with."

Jason chuckled. "Well that's fair enough." He sighed. "So Petey's going to ask me to the dance?"

"On Friday." Val laughed a little. "She's . . .

well, she thinks it'll take her that long to get her nerve up."

"So we've got until Friday to somehow get Petey to feel romantic about David," Jason said.

Val chewed her lower lip. "Listen, Jason, I really don't want to do any more scheming. I've been feeling miserable about deceiving Petey, and I don't want to do it any longer."

"I understand how you feel," Jason said in a comforting tone. "But I'm trying to think of David, too. And I think I've figured out something we could try. Could you come to dress rehearsal tomorrow night?"

"Dress rehearsal?" Val asked. "Yes, I guess I could. I'm supposed to write a review of the play for English, and it probably wouldn't hurt to see it twice. Why do you want me to come?"

"Because David and Petey will both be there," Jason said. "Petey handles the costumes and David runs the lights. If you're there, we might be able to get them alone together for a little while—in a really *romantic* setting."

"Listen, Jason," Val began reluctantly, "maybe if you just said no—in a nice way—she'd just forget about it and ask David to the dance. I'm just not sure we ought to—"

Jason didn't let her finish. "Don't say no,"

he urged. "Think about it overnight. I'll ask you tomorrow morning."

"Okay," Val said after a moment's hesitation. "Jason? Thanks for bringing the daffodil. It was really sweet of you."

"Oh, that's okay," Jason said. His voice softened. "I'm glad you like it. See you tomorrow."

Val went to sleep that night with the yellow daffodil on the table beside her bed and the soft, warm sound of his voice in her ears.

"Dress rehearsal will give you a different view of the play entirely," Petey said as she and Val walked into the auditorium the next night. "You'll get to see us make all our mistakes tonight, so we won't make them opening night."

Val nodded and looked around expectantly. Whatever Jason had up his sleeve, she was glad she had come. She knew that her paper would be much better. Anyway, the evening was going to be interesting—and she'd get to be with Jason.

The auditorium was almost empty and the lights were off. Up on the stage, the footlights were on. Mrs. Buscher, the drama coach, was standing in the front row with her hands on her hips, giving instructions to a stagehand. She turned and smiled as Petey came up to her. "Hello there, Alberta. Are all your costumes ready to go?"

"I'm going to check them now," Petey said, sounding very professional. She gestured at Val. "Is it okay if Val watches rehearsal tonight? She's got to write a review of the play for her English paper."

"Of course." Mrs. Buscher nodded absently and turned back to the stage. "David?" she called. "David MacIntosh, where are you?"

David stuck his head out from behind the set. "Here I am," he answered. He saw Petey and waved at her, a wide smile lighting his face. Petey waved back.

"Why don't you get together with Jason and have a run-through on the lights," Mrs. Buscher said.

"Okay." David disappeared and Jason, dressed in tan cords and a brown-and-gold sweater, came out on the stage, carrying a clipboard under his arm. At the sight of him, Val felt breathless and slightly giddy. She still couldn't believe that he returned her feelings for him. She'd always thought it was just a hopeless crush.

"Jason, will you check David out on the lights?" Mrs. Buscher said. "I'm going to the costume room to check over the makeup."

Mrs. Buscher left and Jason peered out over the footlights. "Hi, Petey," he said. He pretended surprise when he saw Val. "Hi, Val! What are you doing here tonight?"

"She's writing a review of the play for English," Petey explained. "She asked if she could come. Mrs. Buscher just said it was okay."

"Sure it's okay," Jason said. He vaulted lightly off the stage and pointed to the empty front row. "David and I are going to do a run-through on the lights," he said to Val. "Want to watch? Maybe I can explain some of the lighting tricks we're using for the play."

"I'm going to check the costumes," Petey told Val, waving as she turned to go. "The actors will be here in another half hour and I have to have everything ready for them. Come backstage whenever you want."

"I'm glad you decided to come," Jason said as he and Val sat down together. "Let's fix the lights first, and then we can talk." He flipped through some papers on the clipboard, found what he was looking for, and raised his voice. "Okay, David, start your run-through."

For ten minutes or so, David worked with the lights and Jason followed his progress on a sheet of paper, explaining things to Val as they went along. Then, when it was over and David had turned the footlights back on, Jason called out, "Great job, David."

He turned to Val, putting his arm across the back of the seat. "Here's my new plan—"

Val stopped him. "I've decided that this is absolutely our last effort. If this doesn't work, then—" She broke off. If this didn't work, she wasn't sure what would happen next. Would Jason feel obligated to go to the dance with Petey? What would happen after the dance was over? Things were getting so confused.

Jason nodded. "Okay. But see what you think of my idea. There's this big prop closet in the basement where we keep all the stage props we need for the play. The light switch for the room is in the hallway, outside the door. We send Petey to get some props, then we send David, too. The door is kind of heavy and the lock's broken, so there's a stick holding it open. We wait until they're both in the closet, and we knock the stick out so that the door closes. It'll lock. Then all we have to do is leave them in the room for ten or fifteen minutes, and see what happens. I haven't told David any of this, by the way," he added with a grin. "I thought it would be more convincing if it was spontaneous."

Val shook her head dubiously, frowning a little. "Are you sure it'll work?" she asked.

"No, I'm not sure," Jason confessed with a shrug, "but I think it's worth a shot, don't you? What's more romantic than a dark room? If Petey wants romance, we give her romance."

"But Petey might get scared," Val objected.

"I mean, locked up in the dark isn't exactly a fun way to spend fifteen minutes."

"She's not scared of the dark, or claustrophobic, is she?" Jason asked. "If she is, we won't do this." When Val shook her head, he added, "Anyway, she's got David to protect her. What more could a girl want?"

"Well, okay," Val agreed. "What do I have to do?"

"Let's go backstage," he said, pulling Val with him, "and get Petey to go down to the basement."

"Hey, Petey," Jason said when they reached the costume room backstage. "We need some things from the prop closet in the basement. Can you be a sport and go look for them?" He scribbled on a piece of paper on his clipboard, tore off the paper, and handed it to Petey.

"Sure," Petey replied cheerfully, pushing the costume rack back against the wall. "I know every inch of that supply closet. I'll bet I could find stuff down there in the dark." She took the list and scanned it. "Back in a flash," she said, and dashed out the door.

"That was easy," Val said as she and Jason went out into the hall.

"Yeah," Jason replied. "Now for David. We don't want to make this too obvious, just in case the two of them start comparing notes."

David was backstage on a ladder, hammering on one of the sets for the second act. He climbed down off the ladder when he saw Jason, and nodded at Val. "Say, Jason, I've got an idea about the lighting sequences," he said, sticking the hammer in his belt. "For the bus station scene, how about if I bring up a little more blue through the window? That might give it a moonlight effect."

"Sounds good," Jason said. "Actually, lighting might be the last of our worries." He frowned dramatically.

"Got a problem?" David asked.

"I've been looking everywhere for the background tape of nature sound effects for the last act. It seems to have vanished. Do you know where it is? I'll be in deep trouble if we don't find it."

"The tape?" David scratched his head. "Oh, yeah. Well, the last time I saw it, it was on the shelf in the prop closet, down in the basement. Do you want me to get it for you?"

Jason looked grateful. "Would you? I'd go, but the ushers are going to be here in a few minutes, and I've got to talk to them."

Thirty seconds later, Jason put his finger to his lips to warn Val to be quiet, and they tiptoed down the stairs after David. He disappeared through an open door.

"Hi!" Val heard him say. He sounded surprised. "Hey, Petey, what are you doing here?"

"Oh, I'm getting a few props for tonight," Petey responded. "Are you looking for something special?"

"The sound-effects tape for the last act," David replied. It sounded as if he was rummaging around on a shelf. "I know I saw it here on the—"

"Hey!" Petey yelled frantically. There was a crash, as if she'd dropped something on the cement floor. "Get that door!" she shrieked. "It's closing!"

Jason had pushed aside the piece of board that was holding the door, and the heavy door swung shut. There was a loud click as it locked. He signaled to Val, and she switched off the light.

From inside the room, Petey gave a muffled squeal. "The light! What happened to the light?"

"Maybe it burned out," David said. He came to the door and tried to open it. "Hey, the door's locked!" Val heard him exclaim. "It won't open!"

"Of course it's locked, dummy," Petey retorted disgustedly. "The lock's been broken for the past week. That's why that board was holding it open. You can open it from the outside, but you can't budge it from the in-

105

side. We're locked in until somebody comes along and opens it for us!"

"Well," David suggested in a reasonable tone, "why don't we just get comfortable and wait? Somebody's bound to come looking for us sooner or later, and they'll let us out."

Jason took Val's hand. "Let's get out of here!" he said, and they dashed for the stairs.

"How long do we wait?" Val asked breathlessly when they were back upstairs.

"Tell you what," Jason said, looking at his watch, "let's give them about fifteen minutes. I'll go talk to the ushers and make sure they know what they're supposed to do tomorrow night. Then you go let them out."

"Me?" Val squeaked.

"Sure. You can say that you were looking for Petey, and you remembered she'd gone to the prop closet."

It was a long fifteen minutes. Val wandered to the dressing room, where the actors were beginning to gather. A couple of them were already in costume, and one—a girl wearing a gray wig and a frumpy-looking housedress and slippers—was getting made up at the makeup table.

The girl with the gray wig turned around. "I looked for the shawl," she said, "but I can't find it on the rack. Do you know where it is?"

The makeup girl shook her head. "You'll have to ask Petey," she said. She looked around. "She was here a few minutes ago—where did she go?"

"She went down to the prop closet," Val spoke up eagerly. "Something must have delayed her. I'll go tell her she's wanted."

Val went down the basement stairs, listening for sounds of somebody thumping on the prop closet door. But everything was so quiet that she wondered if the plan really had worked. Were Petey and David, sitting there together in the dark, beginning to realize the romantic attraction between them? Val crossed her fingers, hoping desperately that it was true.

She took a deep breath. "Hey, Petey. Are you in there?" she called. "Everyone's been looking for you," she added as she opened the door.

"Finally!" Val heard Petey say with disgust.

It was dark inside, but the light from the hallway was bright enough to show Val what was happening. It was obvious that Petey and David hadn't experienced a romantic interlude. They were sitting stiffly on opposite sides of the little room, and Petey was glaring angrily at David. When she saw Val, she jumped up and hugged her.

"I *knew* you'd come," she said, breathless with relief. "Oh, I'm so *glad* to see you, Val!

We've been stuck in this stupid room for *hours* and *hours*."

David raised one eyebrow and looked at his watch. "Well, for fifteen minutes, anyway," he said mildly. There was a hint of amusement in his eyes.

Petey turned furiously on David. "Don't you fifteen-minute me, David MacIntosh," she yelled. "If it hadn't been for you kicking the stupid door shut, we wouldn't have been locked in here in the first place!"

David was obviously trying to smother a laugh. "But I didn't kick the door shut," he objected.

"And it's *not* funny!" Petey shrieked. She stamped her foot. "It's not funny at all!"

Val sighed. So much for romance.

Chapter Eleven

Back in the auditorium, Val slumped down in a seat in the third row. Mrs. Buscher was having a whispered conversation with Jason in the row in front of her. Then the curtains opened on a cue from Mrs. Buscher, and a radio on a table in the living room set began to play dance music from the 1940's. A gray-haired woman in a housedress and slippers was sitting in a rocking chair, rocking back and forth, knitting and humming to the music.

Jason got up from his seat beside Mrs. Buscher and came to sit next to Val. "How did it go?" he whispered. "Did David and Petey find moonlight and roses in the prop closet? Are they going to live happily ever after?"

"It was a total disaster " Val whispered back

glumly. She couldn't even manage a smile at Jason's joke. "Petey got mad at David because she thought he purposely kicked the door shut. When I got there, she started yelling at him."

"Rats!" Jason exclaimed. He stared at the scene on the stage. A young woman had entered and was arguing loudly with the older woman. "Well," he said after a minute, "I guess that does it, huh?"

"I guess it does," Val said with a sigh. "I'm tired of all these schemes—and anyway, it's just not right to try to get Petey to do something she obviously doesn't want to do." She sneaked a glance at Jason out of the corner of her eye. "Don't you agree?"

"I have one more idea," Jason said.

"But I thought we said—" Val started to object.

Jason put a finger on her lips. "Listen, I'll agree to go to the dance with Petey—*if* you'll ask David to be your date. That way we'll at least be together. And after the dance is over, I'll find a way of telling Petey that *you're* the one I'm interested in."

Val sat up a little straighter. It was a compromise, and one that she didn't want to make. She'd already told Petey that she didn't want to go to the dance with David, and she wasn't sure she could sit by and watch while

Petey and Jason danced together. And how would Petey take it when Jason told her that he wasn't really interested in her—but in her best friend? Would she be angry? Would she feel terribly hurt and cheated? Val shook her head. She couldn't trade Petey's friendship for Jason's heart, no matter how much she cared for him. But maybe she could agree to part of the compromise anyway.

"I'll ask David to the dance," she said finally, "so we can be together. But only on one condition—that we both remember that *Petey* is your date, not I. It wouldn't be fair any other way." She looked up at the stage and swallowed. "And I'm not ready yet to agree that you should tell Petey about us, Jason. I don't want her to be hurt or angry."

Jason looked at her steadily. "Valerie Cassidy, I'd say that you're one friend in a million. I hope Petey knows just how lucky she is."

Val could feel the color rising in her cheeks. Jason was wrong, but she couldn't tell him that. A *real* friend wouldn't have tried to manipulate Petey, the way she had. A real friend would have been honest and aboveboard. There was a long silence before she asked, "Do you think that David will say yes? If I ask him to the dance, I mean."

Jason nodded. "He likes you. And anyway,

if we double-date, he'll get to dance with Petey, you know."

Val managed a laugh. "What a mess," she said. Then, trying to look on the bright side of things, she said determinedly, "I'm sure we'll have a lot of fun."

"That's the spirit," Jason replied, and reached for her hand in the darkness. "Tell Petey tomorrow morning that I'll say yes, and I'll talk to David. Maybe we can get this thing settled."

The next morning, Val dressed for school in her jeans and a blue sweater and black leather boots. While she brushed her dark hair, she looked at herself long and hard in the mirror. She didn't really like what she had been doing to Petey—but she liked Jason *so* much! If only there were a way . . .

In the kitchen, her father was standing by the window, staring out at the falling snow. A three-foot drift had piled up under the willow tree, and the drive was knee-deep in blowing white banks, even though he had shoveled it out the night before. The radio announcer was just finishing the news, and Val's mother switched the radio off as she poured the orange juice into the glasses on the table.

"Have they canceled school?" Val asked, sitting down and drinking her orange juice. She wasn't sure whether to be hopeful or not. If there wasn't any school, she would miss seeing Jason today, and that would be a terrible disappointment. On the other hand, if they called off school, she could put off talking to Petey—and she wouldn't have to ask David to the dance. And that wouldn't be any disappointment at all.

"No, they haven't," Val's mother replied. "They did report that the school buses might be running late, though. The snowplows were out early, but they haven't gotten to some of the roads yet."

"You mean we've got to go to school today?" Wilson began to eat his cereal, looking glum. "I thought maybe I could stay home and make a snowman."

"Too bad, Willie," Mr. Cassidy commiserated. He reached over and ruffled Wilson's hair. "Better luck next time." He sat down on a chair and began to pull on his boots. "Well, if I'm going to get to town, I'd better get the car warmed up."

"Maybe you should take the children to school, Peter," Val's mother suggested. "When it's icy, the way it is this morning, the curves in the hills can be really treacherous. Who knows how long they might have to wait out in the cold for the buses—or how late they might be getting to school?"

"I'll wait," Wilson said with a lopsided smile. "Then I might even get to miss 'rithmetic, and Mrs. Mitchell won't have anybody to tell her what the right number is."

"Oh, horrors!" Val said, reaching over and tickling her brother under the arms. "We can't have you missing 'rithmetic. Come on, Willie, finish your cereal and we'll ride with Dad." She grabbed a hot muffin off the plate and began to eat it hurriedly. If she didn't ride the bus, she could put off talking to Petey until they met at their lockers, before the bell rang. That would certainly be soon enough.

Val's mother went to the phone. "I think I'll call the Boyds and find out whether Petey wants a ride too," she said, picking up the phone and beginning to dial.

"No, don't," Val said, bending over to adjust her boots. She looked up to find her mother giving her a quizzical look. "I mean, Petey likes to ride the bus in the mornings," she added lamely. "She'd probably feel she had to go with us or risk hurting our feelings."

Mrs. Cassidy put down the phone. "Well, if you say so," she said reluctantly, "although it really isn't a good morning to stand out in the snow." She went to the window and looked out. "If this keeps up, they'll have to dismiss school early today."

"They will?" Wilson asked eagerly. "Gosh, then maybe I could miss spelling!"

When Val went outside, the snow was blowing across the lane in flat, sweeping gusts, as if a giant's broom had sent it flying. The wind took Val's breath away as she hurried to the car, and by the time she climbed into the front seat, the sleeves of her red coat were thickly dusted with snow and there were flakes in her hair and on her eyelashes. Wilson got into the back seat, and Mr. Cassidy started the car.

"The worst of this," he said as he steered carefully down the lane, "is that there's still plenty of ice under all this snow. It makes the road awfully slick. There'll probably be a fair number of accidents this morning, especially in the hills."

Val clutched the door handle as the car threatened to skid around the long, steep curve that took them down to the main road. "Just as long as we're not one of them," she muttered as she tightened her seat belt.

The halls were still pretty empty when Val got to school because most of the buses weren't in yet. She wasn't surprised—and not at all disappointed—when Petey didn't appear at the locker before the bell rang for homeroom.

In homeroom, Jason came up to her as she

put her books on her desk. "Have you talked to Petey yet?" he asked.

Val shook her head. "I haven't had a chance. Have you talked to David?"

"His bus isn't in yet."

"Petey rides the same bus," Val reminded him.

"Oh, yeah, that's right." Jason nodded. "I guess we can stop worrying about it for a while, huh?"

But the bus still wasn't in by the end of first period. Val was beginning to feel a nervous churning in the pit of her stomach as she headed to second-period English. She wished this charade was over. She knew it was silly, but she couldn't stand the thought of watching Petey and Jason together at the dance. But the only other real alternative was to confess about this whole mess to her friend, and she wasn't quite ready to do that yet. . . .

"Hey, Val!" Ashley Taft called excitedly as she hurried down the hall after her. "Wait up! I've got to tell you something."

Val hadn't talked to Ashley since the episode with "Tidbits," and she wasn't sure she wanted to. But something in Ashley's tone made her wait.

"Have you heard what happened to Petey's bus?" Ashley asked, out of breath from running.

Val frowned. "Petey's bus?" she repeated. "Well, I know that Petey and the others haven't gotten here yet. I guess the snow has slowed up the bus route."

Ashley's eyes were wide. "They haven't gotten here because—" she paused and made a theatrical gesture, "because the bus was in a *wreck!*"

"A wreck!" Val stared at Ashley, not wanting to believe what she had just heard. "Petey's bus was in accident? Where did you hear this rumor?"

"It's not a rumor!" Ashley straightened her shoulders, looking indignant. "It's the truth! I was in the office, taking a note from Miss Wilson to the secretary, and I overheard the principal talking on the phone to the sheriff's office. She was talking about a school bus that went off the road.'

Val took a deep breath, trying to steady herself. "But how do you know it was *Petey's* bus?" she insisted. "Maybe it was one of the other buses."

"Because," Ashey said, "the principal was reading off the names of the students who were involved—and Petey's name was on the list."

Val sagged against the wall, staring horror-struck at Ashley. She was afraid she was going to be sick. "What . . . how bad was it?" she asked, her voice trembling.

"I couldn't tell from what the principal was saying," Ashley admitted. "But I did hear her say that the bus had turned over, and that they'd called an ambulance. So apparently people were hurt!" she finished excitedly.

An ambulance! They'd taken Petey to the hospital! Val closed her eyes, tightly clenching them shut. If she'd only let her mother call Petey this morning to offer her a ride to school, she wouldn't have been on the bus when it turned over! It was *her* fault that Petey had taken the bus—and if anything terrible had happened to her, that was her fault too! She felt the tears begin to squeeze from under her eyelids and trickle down her cheeks. Petey was hurt, maybe *badly* hurt. Petey was in the hospital—and it was all because of her!

A soft sob escaped from her lips. "Val? Hey, what's the matter?" It was Jason, suddenly standing beside her, and his voice held deep concern. "Why are you crying? Are you hurt?" he asked, taking hold of her arm.

Val opened her eyes. "Have you heard . . . anything about the wreck?" she asked unsteadily, trying to choke back the tears.

"No," Jason said, frowning. He looked at

118

her intently. "What wreck? What are you talking about?"

"The school bus wreck," Ashley interjected. She shifted her books from one arm to the other. "David MacIntosh was in it too, you know."

"David?" Jason asked.

"David?" Val echoed. She stared at Ashley. Of course. The bus had a regular route. It always picked up David first, Petey second. So they would *both* have been aboard when the accident happened.

Jason was making Ashley tell her story all over again. When she got to the part about the ambulance and the hospital, he stopped her and turned to Val. "Are you thinking what I'm thinking?" he asked urgently.

"Yes, I am," Val said. "Please—let's go." And the two of them began to run down the hall as the bell rang for second period.

"But . . . but the bell's ringing," Ashley sputtered, looking annoyed because they hadn't let her finish her story. "It's time for English. Where are you going?"

"Tell Mrs. Hawkins that we've gone to the principal's office to try to find out exactly what happened," Val called back over her shoulder.

In the principal's office, the secretary was on the telephone. After a moment, she put it down and turned to Val and Jason. "Can I help you?" she asked. She looked troubled.

Val stepped to the counter that divided the office. "I hope so," she said, her heart in her mouth. "Do you have any details about the school bus accident that happened this morning?"

The secretary looked from Val to Jason. "I don't think I should—"

"Our *best* friends were on that bus," Jason interrupted. "If we can't find out anything from you, we'll have to go to the hospital." He cleared his throat. "Can't you tell us anything?"

The secretary sighed and her shoulders slumped. "I've been on the phone to the parents," she said. "The only information I have is that the bus went off the road at Shepherd's Creek and rolled over down a steep embankment. The driver was badly hurt, and the kids—there were four of them on the bus—were pretty banged up. Unfortunately, it was quite a while before the emergency crews got there—that's a deserted stretch of road, you know."

Val swallowed hard. Shepherd's Creek was only about five or six miles from her house, in the direction of Anderson Mill. If she'd ridden the school bus this morning, she would have been on it when it went off the road. And the embankment *was* steep, terribly steep, and rocky. She shut her eyes, trying to block out the picture of the yellow bus, rolling over and over, smashing against boulders, while inside . . .

"—think we ought to go to the hospital?" Jason was asking. "It's only a few blocks. We can walk."

With an effort, Val nodded, dazed, still trying to comprehend what had happened. Jason turned to the secretary. "My name is Jason Talbot," he said, "and this is Valerie Cassidy. Please mark us absent. We're going to the hospital."

"I won't have to do that," the secretary said. "We're about to dismiss school. The snow's getting worse, and the principal thinks that everybody ought to go home for the day."

"Thanks," Jason said. He turned to Val and took her hand. "Come on, Val," he said, "let's go."

Chapter Twelve

"I think I'd better call my mother and tell her where I'm going," Val said as they passed the pay phone at the entrance of the school building.

Her mother was very concerned when she heard the news. "I'll call the Boyds right away and see if there's anything I can do. How will you get home from the hospital?"

"I can go to Dad's office," Val said. As she said goodbye, the bell rang and the hallway began to fill with kids, excited to be let out early.

It was only a ten-minute walk to the hospital, but it seemed to Val that it took hours. It was snowing harder than ever, and the wind blew in sharp, icy gusts that took her breath away and made her shiver inside her warm red coat. She pulled her muffler up over her mouth and clenched her mittened fists in her pockets. One thought played over and over again in her head. If only she hadn't been so hung up about her feelings for Jason, she would have asked Petey to ride to school with her, and Petey wouldn't have been on that bus. If only she'd been honest and straightforward and told Petey how she felt about Jason, none of this would have happened. If only she'd been a true friend. . . .

Once, Jason reached out and touched her arm, a look of concern on his face. But Val could only respond with a shake of her head. If Petey was seriously hurt because of her involvement with Jason, she'd never forgive herself. Never!

At the hospital parking lot, they waded through the snow to the emergency room entrance. Inside, there were a half dozen people in the waiting room. Over in the corner, Val saw a woman looking out the window, her back to them.

"There's Petey's mother," Val whispered to Jason, pointing to the woman. "Maybe she knows something about Petey's condition."

Val and Jason started to go over to Mrs. Boyd. But just at that moment, the hallway door burst open, and Petey walked through. She was followed more slowly by David, who was limping and sporting a white bandage on his forearm. Petey saw Val and her mother right away, and waved jauntily.

"Hi, Mom. Hi, Val," she said. "I'm okay. I hope you weren't too worried." She gave Jason an oddly uncomfortable look. "Hi, Jason."

"Petey!" Val cried, breathless with relief. In a second, she'd enveloped her friend in a huge hug. "Worried?" she said. "We were *frantic!*"

Petey's mother hurried forward and embraced her daughter. Then she held her at arm's length and looked at her carefully. "You're really okay, Alberta?" she asked anxiously. "You weren't hurt? How about the others?"

"No, I wasn't hurt at all," Petey said, "not even a scratch, though I'm sure I'll have a few good bruises in a day or two. And the other two students who were cut weren't hurt badly at all—they've already been treated and left. But the driver was hurt, and so was David." She turned to David and drew him forward, giving him an admiring look. "David's arm was cut, a really *deep* cut, and he twisted his ankle. Still, that didn't keep him from being a hero."

David blushed bright red and ducked his head. "Come on, Petey," he muttered, scuffing the toe of his sneaker against the floor, "you don't have to go through the whole thing again, do you?"

"You bet I do," Petey exclaimed proudly. She turned to Val with a dramatic gesture. "Really, Val, you should have seen it—it was awful! The bus went over and over and over, just like a roller coaster doing flips. . . ."

David raised an eyebrow and grinned at Jason. "Actually," he corrected her, "we only rolled once."

Petey made a comic face at him. "Well, it *seemed* like a roller coaster," she insisted. "Anyway, everybody was screaming and yelling, the driver was knocked out and his leg was bleeding, and David just took charge of *everything,* in spite of the cut on his arm. He knew exactly what to do. Why, if he hadn't made a bandage for the driver's leg and stopped the bleeding, he might have bled to death!" She took David's arm and looked up at him with a smile.

Val stared at Petey. She recognized that look—it was an *adoring* look. Petey was looking at David exactly as if she had a major crush on him. She couldn't believe it. After all their scheming to make things happen between David and Petey, and it took an accident to bring them together! There was no understanding love.

"I don't think you ought to make such a big deal about it," David mumbled, looking down again. "It wasn't much."

"Oh, yes, it was, son." A white-coated doctor had come up to join the group. He put a hand on David's shoulder. "Your first aid probably made all the difference for that driver." He looked around at the others. "Because of the road conditions, it took the ambulance a long time to get to the scene of the accident. But when the emergency squad finally did get there, they found that this young man had everything well in hand. He'd quieted the panic among the students and administered first aid not only to the driver but to the other two students who were scratched up. The driver's going to be fine, now that he's getting the blood he needs." He smiled down at Petey. "If you ask me, I'd say that your friend David MacIntosh is a genuine hero."

"I'll say," Petey said proudly, lifting her chin. She grinned at Val. "I can't *wait* to get to school and tell Ashley Taft all about the accident. This time she'll really have a story for the paper. And it'll be the truth, too. She won't have to make *any* of it up!"

Petey's mother shook her head. "I think it would be a much better idea if you didn't go back to school this morning," she said. "Why don't you come home and lie down for a while?"

"Anyway," Val said, "you'll have to wait until Monday to tell your story to Ashley. School is closed and everybody's gone home."

"Oh, fudge," Petey said with a disappointed scowl. "I suppose that means no play tonight, too."

Petey's mother put her arm around Petey's shoulder and smiled at the group. "Well, if I can't talk my daughter into going home for a nap, how about letting me talk all of you into a giant pizza, to celebrate your narrow escape."

"Hey that's great, Mrs. Boyd," David said enthusiastically. He grinned at Val and Jason. "This sure beats going to history class, doesn't it?"

"You bet!" Jason agreed with a secret smile at Val, and they all laughed.

After they finished lunch, Mrs. Boyd dropped Jason off at his house in town and then drove David home. When they got to Val's house, Val invited Petey to spend the afternoon with her. "We can always cut out more of those ridiculous paper hearts," she said with a laugh, as they climbed out of the car.

"Well, actually," Petey said, "there's something I want to talk to you about. Something serious." She knitted her eyebrows together. "Something *really* serious."

"Yeah?" Val said, pulling off her boots on the clean-swept porch. "Me too. There's something I have to tell you." She'd decided during lunch that it was time she came clean. She was tired of keeping secrets from Petey. No matter what happened with Jason and the dance, it would feel very good to get it all out in the open and ask Petey to forgive her.

The front door opened. "Oh, Petey!" Mrs. Cassidy exclaimed delightedly. "I'm so glad to see you all in one piece! How *are* you? Come in and have some hot chocolate."

After Petey had told her story to Val's mother over a steaming mug of hot chocolate, the girls went upstairs to Val's room.

"So who goes first?" Val asked, sitting on her bed and clasping her knees to her chest.

"Me, I guess," Petey said. She sat on the end of the bed and looked uncomfortable. "You know that business about me asking Jason to the dance?"

Val cleared her throat. "Yes," she said, "I know. That's what I want to talk about too. I think I owe you an apology about it. Like maybe a couple of big, fat ones."

But Petey didn't seem to be listening. She was winding a strand of her ponytail around her finger, looking dreamy. "The truth is," she said, "that I've changed my mind. About David, I mean. After what happened this morning, with the accident and all, I can see that *he's* the guy for me."

Val laughed. "I could see by the starry-eyed way you looked at him that he was your hero. And a *romantic* hero, too."

Petey nodded excitedly. "You should have seen the way he acted, Val. I mean, he was *wonderful,* taking charge of things the way he did. Talk about romance? What more could a girl want than somebody like David?" She wrinkled her nose in a frown. "Anyway, that's why I want to ask him to the dance. And that's what I'm worried about."

Val looked at her in astonishment. "Worried? You mean, you're worried that David won't say yes?"

Petey picked at the chenille bedspread. "No, not really." A blush spread over her cheeks. "I mean, I'm pretty sure he likes me—in spite of the fact that I've been behaving sort of like a jerk around him. Like when we were shut in the prop closet and I called him all kinds of names for kicking the door shut and locking us in there. But he says he forgives me for being so silly." She smiled a little, dreamily. "I think if I asked him to go to the dance, he'd say yes right away."

"Well, then," Val demanded, "if you're not worried about David going to the dance with you, what *are* you worried about?"

"It's Jason," Petey said unhappily. "I mean, I've already practically *asked* him to the dance.

You've been talking to him about it for the last week or two, and he knows I was planning to ask—" She broke off suddenly, staring at Val with a suspicious frown. "Hey, how come you're looking at me like that?"

Val took a deep breath, praying that Petey would understand and not be angry. If she didn't tell Petey what had happened, she knew that now she might never find out. But that didn't matter. She had to come clean with her friend. "It wasn't David who kicked the door shut and locked you in the prop closet, Petey," she confessed. "It was Jason. And I'm the one who turned off the lights."

Petey's mouth dropped open. "Jason? And you? You mean . . . you mean, *you* guys locked us in? But why? Was it some kind of a joke?"

"No," Val said, swallowing. "It was all part of a plan."

"Part of a plan?" Petey sat up straighter and her eyes narrowed. "Valerie Cassidy, I think you'd better start at the beginning and go all the way to the end. Without stopping."

"Well," Val said, clasping her hands together to still their nervous shaking, "the whole thing began when you told me that you wanted to go to the dance with Jason." She frowned slightly, concentrating. "No, actually it didn't start there. It started before that, when I decided that *I* wanted to ask Jason to the dance."

Petey stared at her blankly. "You? *You're* interested in Jason? But why didn't you *say* so? Why didn't you tell me?"

"Because I . . . I don't know," Val said. "I mean, at the time I didn't want to talk about how I felt. I figured nothing would come of it, anyway. And then you said you wanted to go with him, and . . ." She shrugged helplessly. "Anyway, that was the beginning. And then when I talked to Jason about you he said he . . ." She swallowed.

"He what?" Petey prompted. "Come on, you've got to tell the *whole* thing."

"He said that he really wanted to go to the dance with me," Val said miserably. "And that David really hoped that you'd ask *him*."

"You're kidding!" Petey exclaimed. "So you thought you'd try to get the two of us together by locking us in the prop closet, huh?"

Val nodded, glad to see that Petey didn't look too angry. "But that wasn't the first time," she admitted. "The first time was when Jason and I changed the computer program so that you and David would get matched up."

"You mean," Petey said, looking disappointed, "that we weren't *really* secret soul mates?"

"Yes, you were—really," Val assured her.

In spite of herself she began to giggle. "You know, that's the funny part of the whole thing. You and David were already paired up—legitimately, I mean. We didn't need to do anything to the program to make that happen. But we sure messed up everybody else's pairing. That's how I got stuck with Ashley Taft."

"It serves you right," Petey laughed. "That's what you get for meddling. It was poetic justice, if you ask me."

"I know," Val said, and then she hesitated. What she had to say next was the most difficult admission. "Actually, Petey, *I'm* the one who's responsible for that item in Ashley's column." She bit her lip. "I'm the anonymous source."

Petey did a double take. "*You* told Ashley Taft that David and I had a secret thing going on?"

"No, not exactly. But I didn't exactly tell her you *didn't*, either." Val looked at Petey contritely. "If you're going to be mad and never forgive me, I'll understand. It definitely *was* a rotten thing to do."

"Yeah, it was," Petey said sternly. She frowned at Val for a few seconds, and then her face relaxed. "But don't forget that I know Ashley Taft too. It's pretty hard to tell her she's wrong about something when she's made up her mind that she's right."

Val stared at her. "You mean, you're really not mad at me?"

"Not enough to matter. After all, look how everything turned out." Petey leaned forward eagerly. "Are you and Jason *still* . . . I mean, does he still want to go to the dance with you?"

Val nodded. And she couldn't help it—a warm smile lit her face.

"Oh, Val, that's great!" Petey said, clapping her hands together. "That solves my problem perfectly!"

"Huh?"

"Sure. I was worried that Jason expected *me* to ask him to the dance! But if he wants to go with *you*, and you want to go with *him*, then everything's settled!" She got up and threw her arms ecstatically around Val and they both collapsed on the bed, laughing.

"I've really learned something from this mess," Val said seriously when they'd calmed down a bit. "Schemes never really work—they always backfire in the end! We should always just try to be honest with each other."

"I agree," Petey said. "But think of this escapade we'd have missed!" The girls hugged again, dissolving into giggles.

"Hey, you know what?" Petey added when they'd both gotten their breath.

"No, what?" Val asked, with a hiccup.

"We can still make it a double date to the dance," Petey said, grinning. "We've just traded guys, that's all."

"No, we've traded hearts," Val corrected her.

"Yes," Petey agreed, her voice soft. "We've traded hearts."

It was the night of the dance, and Val and Petey were in the girls' restroom, freshening their makeup.

"You know," Petey said, putting away her lipstick and searching through her purse for her blush, "I can't believe that we actually cut out all those stupid hearts, all by ourselves. Did you see? They've got them strung up *everywhere.*"

"*I* believe it," Val laughed, flexing her fingers. "My hands are still sore. Listen, Petey, the next time you get the urge to volunteer our services, how about baking cookies instead?" She looked in the mirror and adjusted the wide belt of her new pink lace dress. It was the prettiest dress she'd ever had, she thought. "Speaking of hearts," she added, re-pinning the pink and white flowers that Jason had given her for her hair, "how have you and David been getting along for

134

the last few days? Has the romance worn off yet?"

A starry look came into Petey's eyes. "Wasn't I silly?" she said softly. "I mean, thinking that David wasn't romantic. You know, tonight when he came to pick me up he brought me two red rosebuds." She blushed. "He said they symbolized our feelings for each another."

"There, you see?" Val said. "It just goes to show that you just can't tell when romance is going to strike next."

"Right," Petey agreed with a grin, putting away her cosmetics. "Rainbows and daffodils, here we come."

"And rosebuds," Val reminded her.

"Right," Petey said again. "And rosebuds. That's what we get for trading hearts."

When they went out on the gym floor, the boys were waiting, and Val went happily into Jason's arms.

"Ah," he said with a sigh as he pulled her out onto the floor, "the moment I've been waiting for." He smiled, looking down at her, and his arms tightened around her shoulders in a way that made her shiver with delight. "You and Petey were gone for a long time. What were you talking about?"

Val laughed lightly. The band was playing her favorite song, and she and Jason moved so easily together that it almost felt as if they were floating.

"Oh, just about rainbows and daffodils," she said. "And trading hearts."

Jason pulled her closer. "The only heart I'm interested in trading for," he said huskily, "is yours. What do you think?"

"I think," Val said as his lips tenderly brushed hers, "that it sounds like a wonderful trade."